The Vampire Stalker

The Vampire Stalker

ALLISON VAN DIEPEN

◪ SCHOLASTIC

For those of you who have ever fallen in love
with a character in a book.

Scholastic Children's Books
An imprint of Scholastic Ltd
Euston House, 24 Eversholt Street
London, NW1 1DB, UK
Registered office: Westfield Road, Southam,
Warwickshire, CV47 0RA
SCHOLASTIC and associated logos are trademarks and/or
registered trademarks of Scholastic Inc.

First published in the US by Scholastic Inc, 2011
This edition published in the UK by Scholastic Ltd, 2011

Text copyright © Allison van Diepen, 2011

The right of Allison van Diepen to be identified as the
author of this work has been asserted by her.

ISBN 978 1407 12989 1

A CIP catalogue record for this book is available from the British Library.

Printed and bound by CPI Group (UK) Ltd, Croydon, CR0 4YY
Papers used by Scholastic Children's Books are made from
wood grown in sustainable forests.

1 3 5 7 9 10 8 6 4 2

This is a work of fiction. Names, characters, places, incidents
and dialogues are products of the author's imagination or are used
fictitiously. Any resemblance to actual people, living or dead,
events or locales is entirely coincidental.

www.scholastic.co.uk/zone

One

There was a festive vibe in the air that reminded me of the Fourth of July. Except I didn't get *this* excited on the Fourth of July.

Today was the day I had waited a whole year for. I was finally going to get my hands on a copy of *The Mists of Otherworld*, a book so hotly anticipated there'd been a whole news segment about it on TV last night.

I stood in the line outside the Book Nook with my best friends, Luisa and Katie. We'd been there since 7:45 a.m. – brutal for a Saturday morning, but worth it – wanting to get a good spot in line before the store opened at nine. The atmosphere was electric. Besides dozens of teenage girls, there were women in their twenties, moms with strollers, a few grandmas, and a handful of teenage guys.

Luisa stepped away from the line and glanced ahead. "I wish they'd let us in already!" She stumbled a little and grabbed Katie's arm for support. Believing that her shortness was a curse, Luisa insisted on wearing the highest wedges Payless had to offer. The result was that she rolled an ankle at least once a month.

"I just hope they don't sell out before we get to the front," I said.

Luisa's brown eyes widened. "Amy! They *can't* sell out — you preordered for us, didn't you?"

"Yeah, but I heard on the news last night that some of the shipments were delayed," I replied, feeling nervous as I spoke the words. The idea that I would have to wait another day to read about Alexander Banks — the gorgeous, fearless vampire hunter — was too awful to contemplate.

"I *am* getting a book today, even if I have to bodycheck someone to get it," Katie announced.

We laughed, because Katie would never hurt a fly — literally. When I'd visited her at the camp where she worked over the summer, she'd ushered even the smallest bugs out the cabin door. However, she *was* five foot ten and the captain of the girls' ice hockey team, so a body check or two wasn't out of the question.

"All I know is, we *have* to read it by Monday morning," I said.

Katie and Luisa nodded. If we didn't finish it by then, we'd have to cover our ears in the spoiler-filled hallways of our school. There had only been one book so far — *Otherworld* — in Elizabeth Howard's planned trilogy, but it was a sensation, and most people we knew had been sucked in.

I felt the cool breeze on my face, and looked around at the swaying trees, appreciating the crisp autumn weather. Some would say it was a waste of a beautiful day, because I planned to spend it inside reading *The Mists of Otherworld*. But sometimes it was nice to read on a lovely day, especially when the world inside the book was so dark and gloomy.

One of the best things about the series was that it was set in my city, Chicago. But Otherworld Chicago was very different from the Chicago I knew. It was a place where mortals stayed in their homes after nightfall. A place where you didn't trust anyone who wasn't your kin.

And it was all because of vampires. As the series told it, for centuries, vampires had existed in isolation in northern Scandinavia, preying on the residents of remote villages. Then in the 1920s, the vampires had decided to leave seclusion and migrate all over the world, creating more vampires as they went along.

Otherworld Chicago had been hit especially hard because one of the world's most notorious vampires, Vigo Skaar, had moved there with his coven of several hundred vampires. Vigo, and his vicious second-in-command, Leander, had been terrorizing the city ever since. As a result, innovation had stopped completely, and Otherworld had not made any technological advancements since the 1920s.

The line surged forward, a sign that the store was opening its doors, and there was a chorus of squeals and some jostling.

Luisa frowned at Katie. "It's going to be a stampede. I told you we should have come earlier!"

Katie shook her head, her blonde ponytail swinging. "I don't wake up before six for *anyone*, not even James Banks."

"How dare you, Katherine? And you think yourself worthy of James!" Luisa made a show of hoisting her chin and turning her back on Katie. A self-professed drama geek, she loved using Otherworld's formal language.

While my Otherworld crush — well, more like obsession — was Alexander Banks, Katie and Luisa loved James, Alexander's golden-haired cousin. Alexander was dark and brooding, and determined to hunt down Vigo, who had murdered his family when Alexander was only six. James was a philosopher who wanted to bring peace to Otherworld. He was in love with Hannah Skaar, Vigo's sister, a vampire whose beauty and feistiness were only matched by her undying love for James.

James was nice to read about, but he was no Alexander. I preferred a guy with some grit.

"I wonder if Alexander is going to fall in love in this book," Katie said as we inched closer to the door. "It's about time, don't you think?"

"Not necessarily," I said, feeling a blush burn my cheeks. I wasn't sure I wanted a love interest for Alexander. The thought of being jealous of a character in a book was silly, but I couldn't help it. Alexander Banks was the closest to perfection that any guy could ever be. What girl could measure up? "He isn't the romantic type. Alexander's too focused on revenge to fall in love."

"Good point," Luisa agreed. A few eager fans were now leaving the store, books in hand, bumping into us because they'd started reading already. "But you never know. If he kills Vigo, he's going to need a new story line."

Just the mention of Vigo gave me chills. There was no doubt in my mind that Alexander would kill Vigo. It was a question of *when*, not *if*.

Finally, it was our turn. As we stepped over the threshold into the Book Nook, I couldn't help but think of how lucky I was that my friends shared my passion for Otherworld. It was actually our love of books that had first brought us together, in the ninth grade. Katie had started a high school book club, and Luisa and I had been the only ones to show up. I'd just moved to the east side of Chicago after my parents' divorce and didn't know anyone. Within weeks, we'd become a "trio of awesomeness", as Katie put it. Most people we met thought we'd been best friends *for ever*, not just for a couple of years.

Thankfully, the three copies I had preordered were there waiting for us. I picked up my book, hugging it to my chest like a long-lost friend. It was extremely thick, longer even than the first, and that made my heart pound: the more Alexander to read about, the better. Katie and Luisa were busy exclaiming over the cover – it had been revealed online months ago, but it was still amazing to see it for real.

The three of us left the store, breathless with triumph. There was no talk of hanging out afterward. We caught the bus and grabbed seats, reading the whole way. When it got to my stop, I reluctantly tucked the book under my arm (since I hadn't mastered reading and walking like Katie had), and waved goodbye to my friends.

My building was called Courtyard Place, a name that made it seem posh when it was anything but. I wouldn't have any complaints about where we lived if it weren't for the fact that my dad and his girlfriend – the one he'd left Mom for – had managed to buy a bungalow in the suburbs. If he could afford to live in a house, why couldn't we?

I pushed those thoughts away, determined not to stew in bitterness. Besides, nothing could shake my good mood today. I had a date with Alexander Banks, after all.

I had to remind myself of that when I got inside the apartment and saw my younger sister, Chrissy, and her best friend, Madison, in the living room.

"Hey," I said.

Chrissy grunted and Madison said, "Hello there." Madison had a way of talking down to people that made me clench my teeth.

I noticed Mom's coat was gone. "Where's Mom?"

"She got called in," Chrissy replied. "Some idiot swallowed a plastic fork on a dare, so they had to open up the clinic."

Mom was an endoscopy nurse – a pretty good gig after toughing it out for fifteen years in the ER. She didn't have to work overnights any more, but she still got called in for emergencies.

"Hope you got your vampire book," Chrissy said, and I caught the *Isn't she pathetic?* glance she and Madison exchanged.

Madison and Chrissy were often mistaken for sisters because they used the same blonde hair dye. They were in eighth grade, but probably looked older than me, and I was a junior. On any given day they dressed like they'd just walked out of a dance club, with their skintight camis, low-slung jeans, and heavy make-up.

If you looked closer, though, Chrissy and I did look like sisters. We were both fair skinned and green eyed, with slightly upturned "snob" noses, as Madison had once pointed out. She'd also pointed out, right in front of me, that Chrissy and I were like *Before* and *After* makeover pictures. I didn't have to ask which one I was. My long, straight hair was the same mousy brown as Chrissy's roots, and I didn't wear make-up most of the time — both capital crimes, in Madison's eyes.

Whatever.

I grabbed a Coke from the fridge and a crumpled bag of trail mix, then went to my room. Kicking off my shoes, I sat back against the pillows, ready to lose myself in *The Mists of Otherworld*.

Hands tingling with anticipation, I opened the book.

———

I slammed the book shut. "No, no, no!"

This was *not* the ending I'd been hoping for.

It was Sunday night just after eleven. I'd been reading all weekend with short breaks for food, hygiene, fresh air, and phone debriefs with my friends.

How could the author leave Alexander's life in the lurch? Hadn't he been through enough already?

Alexander had been more amazing than ever in *The Mists*. But right now, he could be cornered by Vigo and other hungry vampires. And I had to wait another whole year to find out what happened to him! It was so unfair.

A horrible thought occurred to me: she wouldn't kill him off, would she?

No, she wouldn't dare. Alexander was too important. Readers would never forgive her. *I* would never forgive her.

But Elizabeth Howard was notorious for doing things *her* way, no matter what her publisher or fans wanted. I flipped the book over, my fingers sliding over the glossy jacket. Alexander and James were on the cover, with Hannah standing between them and Vigo watching from the shadows. The images on the books' covers were drawn by Howard herself because she felt only she could depict the characters accurately. She had also refused to sell the movie rights, claiming that no actors could be true to her characters. Despite the uproar from fans, I agreed with her on that one. I couldn't imagine anyone doing justice to Alexander Banks.

Sliding off my bed, I crossed to the window, gazing down at

the dark streets below. Our third-floor apartment had a better view now that the project next door had been torn down. From my window I could see most of the neighbourhood, the streets glistening with new rain, mist rising from the sewers.

I could almost hear the sound of Alexander's booted footsteps as he ran down the street, stake in hand, looking for a flash of Vigo's silver-blond hair in the moonlight. If I could spot Alexander in this maze of streets, I'd climb down the fire escape and help him.

Not that I'd be of much use against a vampire.

Anyway, now that I'd finished the book, it was time to go online and vent. I wished I could call Katie or Luisa, but it was too late, and I didn't know if they'd finished the book yet. Turning away from the window, I headed to the computer, which was located in the small den next to the living room.

Chrissy was on the computer.

"What are you up to?" I asked casually, leaning in the doorway. I could see that she was IMing with someone, but she always got defensive if I asked her who it was.

"Madison and I were figuring out which party to go to next Friday," she replied, turning around.

Which party. Of course.

"I guess you're going to the dance," she said in a mocking tone, like a school dance was too cheesy for her. I should just be grateful she wasn't planning to go; I knew she could score tickets if she wanted.

I shrugged. "We'll probably go."

"Madison and I are all about house parties. They're way more fun."

I saw the challenge in her eyes. Chrissy was daring me to say that she should stay away from those parties, that she was too young, and that Madison was a bad influence. At which point she would tell me that a) I wasn't Mom, so stay out of it, and b) I was just jealous of her wonderful social life.

For some reason, Chrissy loved to taunt me these days. We'd been close growing up — with the usual sister squabbles — but since Mom and Dad's separation, Chrissy had turned on me. I guess she had to release her anger somehow, and I was an easy target.

"Are you almost finished with the computer?" I asked.

She sighed, disappointed that I didn't engage her. "Just a minute." She logged off Facebook with one hand and dialled her cell phone with the other, then got up. Mom insisted that we have cell phones for safety reasons. We were all on her phone plan and got free evenings and weekends, which meant that Chrissy was almost always on the phone when she was at home.

I plunked down in the chair and went to my favorite Otherworld fan site, then logged into the readers' forum as MrsAlexanderBanks8021. It was weird to think that there were eight thousand and twenty MrsAlexanderBanks before me. Obviously they all recognized that he was the most incredible character ever. I didn't know why most girls preferred the thoughtful, sensitive James to Alexander. It was a no-brainer.

I began typing.

MrsAlexanderBanks8021: (*Spoilers*) I just finished *The Mists*. I can't believe she ended it with Alexander chasing Vigo! Does anyone here think she might kill off Alexander in the next book? I'm really worried.

I waited, and a reply came up almost instantly:

ILoveJames4ever222: I wouldn't be surprised if she killed him. It doesn't look like he's destined to find happiness. If he were going to have a happy ending, he would've met a girl by now.

At this point, others began chiming in.

JamesBanksmylove9648: She wouldn't dare kill him. She knows we'd all freak out! I heard she's having writer's block and hasn't started the third book yet. Maybe she doesn't know what to do with Alexander.

Writer's block? I thought with dread. I began typing again.

MrsAlexanderBanks8021: I hope she gets over the writer's block soon because one year is way too long for the next book. I can't picture waiting any longer than that.

ElizabethHowardfan4307: I think she'll probably have Vigo kill Alexander. James will go ballistic and get all violent for a change. If James the pacifist kills Vigo, it would be the perfect ending to the series!

A flurry of comments came up, most of them saying that it would be a terrible ending. As if killing off Alexander would work. As if James's personality would do a one-eighty.

I had a sinking feeling in the pit of my stomach. If Alexander died, it meant the end of the fantasy, and that would be too much to bear.

Vigo Skaar looked out of the window of his hiding place, a basement in an abandoned house. Scanning the streets with his pale eyes, he assured himself that he had nothing to worry about. Alexander Banks could not possibly have tracked him here. The vampire stalker was good, but not that good.

He was hungry, so very hungry. But hunting wasn't easy when he, himself, was being hunted.

He stepped back from the window and went to sit down in a battered old armchair, one of the many reminders of the previous inhabitants. When people left town these days, it was usually in a hurry. So many lovely houses allowed to rot because of us, *he thought proudly.*

If Alexander thought he could outsmart him, he would be disappointed. As always, it came down to the calculation of probabilities – something he doubted Alexander understood. Probabilities of where to run, matched with measured risks.

That was one thing Vigo was excellent at: anticipating Alexander's next move.

Sometimes he rather enjoyed their game. Other times, like now, Alexander was a damned nuisance. He wished he'd just killed the lad when he'd had the chance. But then, if he'd known that young Alexander was present when he was killing the boy's family, he would have.

Vigo felt the hairs on the back of his neck rise, and he bolted out of the chair, assuming a fight-ready stance. His predator was approaching. Vigo felt the blood hunger rumble in his belly. A predator who would soon become his prey. . .

I stared at the screen, chewing my bottom lip. The predator-prey thing was overdone these days. So was the cat and mouse thing, come to think of it. I deleted the last line and skimmed over the scene.

Reading *The Mists of Otherworld* tonight had filled me with creative juice. I just had to end the Vigo/Alexander story line once and for all – with Alexander prevailing, of course. I was excited to post it on a fan fiction website and hoped other fans liked it, too.

It was 12:34 a.m., definitely time to stop for the night. I'd stayed up late writing too many times, then ended up headachy the next day. The problem was, I was a night person, and that's when I did my best work.

I'd been writing for as long as I could remember, but once I read *Otherworld*, I'd stopped writing original stories to focus on fan fiction. It was such a rich, exciting world that I couldn't think of writing anything else.

I knew that if I was going to be a writer, I'd have to write my own original stuff one day. It was just too bad that the character of Alexander Banks had already been created by Elizabeth Howard. I wished he was all mine.

$\mathcal{T}$wo

On Monday, as soon as the bell rang for lunch, I stopped in to visit one of my best buddies: the school librarian.

Ms Parker was a middle-aged African-American woman with salt-and-pepper braids and stylish glasses. She favoured colourful cardigans, flowing skirts, and green tea. Like my friends and me, she was a reading addict, and seemed to have a book permanently attached to her left hand.

"You finished it, didn't you?" she asked. Ms P was also a fan of the Otherworld series, which made her the coolest librarian ever.

"I can't believe it ended like that!" I cried, slumping down in the chair next to her desk. I had already discussed the ending with Katie and Luisa on the bus to school that morning. Both my friends were equally outraged by the cliffhanger, although they weren't as worried about Alexander's fate as I was. Luisa speculated that Vigo wouldn't kill Alexander, but turn him into a vampire instead. The idea made me shudder; Alexander hated vampires so much that if he became one, he might stake himself.

"I know," Ms P said, closing out an email and turning to face me. "But it made you eager for the last book in the series, didn't it? I thought Elizabeth Howard did an excellent job of keeping her audience on the edge of their seats."

"You're right," I admitted. "I just don't enjoy being on the edge of my seat for an entire year."

At that, she laughed.

Ms P had started at my high school the year before I entered ninth grade, and she'd had her work cut out for her. Most of the library's collection was more than forty years old. Ms P used whatever money she could get her hands on to buy books, and she displayed the newest, shiniest ones at the front of the library to draw the students in. She went to as many book fairs as possible to score free books, and even wrote to publishers asking for sample copies.

If anyone was a born librarian, it was Ms P, which is why I'd been so surprised to learn that it hadn't been her original career goal. She actually had a master's degree in physics, of all things, and had been ready to start her PhD when fate – or, rather, her love of books – called her in a different direction.

"I'm scared Elizabeth Howard's going to kill off Alexander," I said. "Some people online are saying it. You don't think she would do that, do you?"

"Who knows what an author is thinking? My guess is that she loves Alexander as much as we do. He adds so much excitement to the story, while James can be a little verbose – though I wouldn't dare say that in front of Katie and Luisa," Ms P added, her eyes sparkling. "The thing is, Alexander is a very dark character. She might see him as a tragic figure. Time will tell."

"Come on, you have some connections with the publishing people, right? Can't you draw up a petition with your librarian friends asking Elizabeth Howard to hurry up with Book Three and keep Alexander alive?"

She smiled. "That's a thought. In the meantime, I have another book for you, hot off the press."

There was nothing like being the first to read a new book without having to pay for it. If I liked it enough, I'd go buy it myself. But I'd had to hold off on all book buying lately (except for *The Mists*, of course) because the coffee shop I'd worked at for a year had gone out of business back in August. I'd done several résumé blitzes since then, but had come up with nothing.

Ms P whipped the book out from under the counter with a flourish. It was the new Sheila Katz book. Her light, funny chick-lit novels appealed to my whimsical side. "I thought it would be a nice change of pace from Otherworld," she explained.

"Thanks, Ms P. I'll take good care of it." After she scanned the bar code and my library card, I put the book in my bag.

"So, Amy. Other than your worries about Alexander Banks, is everything going OK?" Ms P had a motherly way of asking you questions, another thing I loved about her. If you wanted to talk, you talked. And if you didn't, she didn't push you. She always let you know the door was open.

There were lots of things I could tell her. Like how Chrissy was driving me crazy these days. Like how my dad hardly ever called, and I'd stopped caring if he did. But there wasn't any point, or anything she could do.

"Yeah, things are OK."

Ms P gave me a knowing look, but didn't pry. "Are you looking forward to the dance this Friday?"

"A little," I said with a shrug. I knew that Katie and Luisa were probably discussing the dance right now at our table in the cafeteria. Luisa would want to figure out our outfits, and Katie would want to dissect who was going with whom. None of us had dates.

Unlike my friends, I'd never had a boyfriend. I'd had a crush here and there, but it never came to anything. Luisa had had several boyfriends, and Katie, who was übershy with guys, dated a guy at camp two summers ago. All I had was a *blah* sort of kiss from one of Luisa's many cousins at her birthday party last year. He never called, and I never cared.

Although I'd never admit it to anyone, reading *The Mists* had left me with an intense longing. *What would it be like,* I wondered, *to date someone like the smouldering Alexander Banks?*

As the week went on, Katie and Luisa's excitement about the dance began to feel contagious. The weather was cold and grey every day, so I would come straight home from school, do homework, and write fan fiction. By Friday night, I was more than ready to go out. My secret, romantic self hoped that some cute guy from another school would show up at the dance and spot me in the crowd. It never happened, of course, but I made sure I looked good just in case. This meant putting some product in my damp hair (Chrissy would have been thrilled), applying some make-up (ditto), and wearing a wispy, girly shirt Luisa had got me for my birthday. Katie, Luisa and I got ready together at Katie's house, and rode the bus to school.

The gym was already packed when we arrived. Beyoncé's new single was playing, so we headed straight for the dance floor. When it ended, another equally awesome song came on. It felt good to get lost in the music and I spun around, my hair fanning out around me.

"Hi, girls!" Ms P infiltrated our triangle, waving her arms above her head to the beat of the music.

A few people laughed and pointed at us. OK, so maybe it wasn't cool to be seen dancing with the school librarian. But I didn't care. Some people were cool no matter what age they were. Ms P was one of those people.

She danced with us until the end of the song, then headed back to her post at the gym doors. She still grooved, though, clapping her hands and swaying her hips, her full skirt sweeping the floor. I had to laugh. She didn't seem to care that our uptight principal, Mr Matthews, was standing ramrod straight beside her.

By the time a slow song came on, I was thirsty, and Luisa said her feet were killing her. We headed towards the vending machines at the back of the gym. Luisa kept tripping in her sky-high wedges, so we were walking very slowly.

We bought sodas, and Luisa leaned back against the wall, taking the weight off her feet. "I hope Jake gets here soon – there's only an hour left to the dance," she said irritably, opening her can of Coke and taking a sip.

"He's not coming," Katie told her. "There's a track meet this weekend."

Luisa had been obsessing over Jake Levine for years. Katie always bugged her to ask him out already – as much for our sanity as for hers – but Luisa had never made a move. I secretly thought that was for the best. Jake was good-looking, sure, but I didn't like him *or* his friends, AKA the jock squad, which included Brian Kowalski, Reuben Torres and Tommy Baird. Those guys acted like they ruled the hallways (which, I guess, they did) and were God's gift to girls (which they definitely *weren't*).

"Jake is not the only cute guy at this school," I pointed out.

"Um, yes, he is," Luisa replied, rolling her eyes. "OK, Amy. If you think there are so many cute guys around, I dare you to ask one to dance."

"No, thanks." As my gaze skimmed over the dance floor, I realized that no one here inspired any excitement in me. How sad that I felt more of a connection to a fictional character than to a guy in real life.

After chatting for a few more minutes, we headed back to the dance floor. The sodas had given us a new kick of energy. Luisa took off her wedges and danced barefoot, swinging her shoes around, but yelped when someone stepped on her foot.

By the time another set of slow songs came on, we decided to get going. The dance would be ending soon, anyway, so we figured we'd beat the coat-check rush. Unfortunately, a bunch of other people had the same idea.

"See you Monday, Ms P," I said, catching her in the midst of a yawn as we filed out of the gym.

"Do any of you girls need a ride home?" she asked.

"Nah, we're good," I said for all of us. The bus ride was part of the fun — that's where we'd rehash the night's events. Not that anything exciting had happened, but we'd find something to talk about.

We picked up some snacks at the deli across the street before boarding the bus with a crowd of people from our school. The freshmen gathered at the back, shouting, tossing food wrappers, and sloshing drinks at one another. The bus driver told them to settle down. I realized that come next year, Chrissy would be among them.

I was the first of my friends to get off the bus. A few other kids got off at the same time, which was good because the area wasn't the most welcoming late at night. It was only a five-minute walk to my building, but the heavy post-rain fog made it seem further away.

I walked quickly, eager to get past the park. Pleasant Park was the city's attempt to green up the area by planting some trees and bushes. A couple of dilapidated buildings had been torn down, and a basketball court, play structure, and swing set had been put in. It was deserted at this time of night, and the sight of it wrapped in fog was creepy.

Suddenly something slammed into my windpipe, cutting off my air. My body reeled with the force of impact. I caught a glimpse of blond hair inches from my face, heard a vicious snarl. *I'm being attacked*, I realized, frozen with horror. An arm snaked around me and then I was moving so fast it felt like I was flying through the air.

A dark figure leaped from the shadows and grabbed my attacker, who was forced to drop me to the ground. I scrambled to my feet and started to run. I could hear blows, grunts, and a sick, almost inhuman growl. A high-pitched screaming filled my ears; it was coming from me.

"Are you all right, madam?" Someone had run up beside me, a long coat flapping in the wind. "Are you injured?"

I stopped running. A nearby streetlight illuminated the fog, giving me a glimpse of the guy's face. He looked very familiar, but I couldn't place him.

"Where'd he go?" I gasped, shaking. I scanned the bushes, terrified my attacker would jump out at any second.

"Ran off. I could not catch him."

Catch him? This guy had to be crazy to think about running after my attacker.

I glanced at him, and felt like the air had been sucked out of me.

His profile was straight and chiselled. Dark brown hair curled slightly over the collar of his long, cape-like coat. A line from *Otherworld* came to mind: *He would have been classically handsome were it not for the forbidding expression on his face.*

I gave my head a shake. Jeez. After all I'd just been through, I was still thinking of Alexander. I did a double take, but his face and figure were now shrouded in darkness and mist. It must have been a mirage – my mind's way of bringing me comfort after the terror.

With trembling hands, I pushed the wild strands of hair out of my face. I didn't know who, or what, had just attacked me, and I had no idea who my saviour was. All I knew was, I had to get home.

"I will show you to your door, miss," the guy said. "Is this the way?"

I looked around, confusion muddling my brain. I was at the other end of the park, where the sandboxes and swing sets were located. How did I get all the way over here? I couldn't have run this far.

It took me a few moments to orient myself. "It's on the other side of the apartment complex."

I practically had to run to keep up with him, while at the same time scanning the darkness for signs of another attack.

"I'm lucky you were there," I said, still trying to catch my breath.

"It was not luck," he said tightly. "I was tracking him. And about to pounce on him before he grabbed you, I might add. I cannot imagine what possessed you to break curfew and leave yourself so exposed. There is no excuse for such recklessness."

I was dumbstruck. He was blaming *me* for getting attacked? "I wasn't breaking my curfew. I don't even have a curfew." Mom had never needed to impose one on me. Chrissy, of course, was a different story.

He shot me a glare. "Indeed? I wonder if the town council would confirm that."

I had no idea what he was talking about, or why he was speaking in such a weird, formal way, but I didn't care to ask. I had bigger problems. We'd reached my building, and I practically dived for the heavy glass door. "I'm going to call the police." I fished in my pocket for the key. "I hope you can give them a better description than I can." My fingers closed around the key, but my hand was shaking so hard that it took several attempts to fit it in the lock.

"Call the police? Are you mad? They are of no use against him. They are too afraid themselves."

I turned to look at him. The area was well lit, and for the first time, I could see him clearly.

And it hit me — again — how much he resembled Alexander Banks, right down to the stony expression he wore on the cover of *The Mists*.

"Look," I said. "I don't know why you were following that guy, but you shouldn't put yourself in danger. He could really hurt you." I was finally able to unlock the door, and I quickly stepped into the lobby.

"I have every intention of killing him before he can do so," he said, following me inside.

His sharp tone unsettled me. Was this guy a vigilante or something? I'd leave that to the police to find out.

I took out my cell phone and turned it on.

"What is *that*?"

"A cell phone," I said slowly, wondering what this guy's deal was. A chill crept down my spine. Maybe I shouldn't have allowed him inside my building.

"Do you mean a telephone? That is very odd, Miss. . . Forgive me, I did not catch your name."

"Amy Hawthorne," I replied automatically.

"I am Alexander Banks." He bowed. "At your service."

$\mathcal{T}$hree

I STARED AT HIM for a few seconds, stunned by his pitch-perfect performance. Then I started to laugh. I couldn't help it.

This guy had *deliberately* done himself up to resemble Alexander Banks. The windswept hair was one thing – lots of guys were adopting that style these days to get girls' attention. But the whole outfit, including the coat and high leather boots . . . it was an Alexander Banks costume.

Leave it to me to be rescued by some Otherworld-obsessed weirdo.

"What is so humorous?" he demanded, arching a dark eyebrow.

"You look a lot like him; I'll give you that."

"A lot like whom?"

"You know, Alexander Banks from the Otherworld books."

He looked puzzled. "I do not know what books you speak of. In any case, I must be off to the Byward District to see if I can pick up his trail. Do you know, perchance, how I can get there from here?"

The Byward District. It was the notorious area of Otherworld Chicago where the vampires congregated at night before prowling the city in search of prey.

I didn't know why he felt he had to continue the joke. I felt an uneasy twist in my stomach. Something was definitely off about this guy. "I'm sorry, but I'm not into the role-playing thing. I'm a fan of the books, too, but I need to deal with the police right now." I turned to walk to the elevator.

"You will offer me no help?" he asked.

I looked back at him again. Seeing the intensity in his eyes, I felt a frisson of fear. "My mother's waiting for me upstairs and could be down any second. And there's a security camera over there." I pointed to it, perched above the mirror to our right. I caught a glimpse of myself and the Alexander look-alike looming in front of me.

He seemed confused. "Only minutes ago, I saved your life, and now you act as if I am threatening it?"

"That man wasn't necessarily going to. . ."

"Vigo Skaar never leaves his victims alive."

Something stilled inside me.

No, this is ridiculous. He's just trying to freak you out.

And it was working.

"Vigo's just a character in a book, OK?" I stepped into the elevator and pressed the button for the third floor, but jumped back when a booted foot lodged itself in the door. It automatically reopened.

"Not so fast." His dark eyes were penetrating. "Not until you explain why you doubt who I am."

I stepped out of the elevator right away. This guy was getting scarier by the minute, and I'd always had a fear of being cornered in an elevator. At least in the lobby, someone might come in. And the threat of the security camera might make him think twice if he had any intention of hurting me.

"Why don't we sit down," he said. It was clearly not a question.

When he took my arm, I didn't resist. I let him walk me over to the sagging chintz couch. He sat down next to me.

"I would like to know why you do not believe what I'm telling you."

I inched away from him as subtly as I could. "I don't know what to say. I told you I just want to call the police."

"And I told *you*, the police are ineffective. Rather than patrolling the streets at night, they adhere to the curfew. They are not qualified to take on Vigo and his coven. This cannot be news to you."

He genuinely seemed to believe what he was saying, which only left one option: he was crazy. I didn't see any choice but to play along. "Yeah, I guess you're right. Anyway, if you want to get to the Byward District, it's just, uh, a couple of miles north of here. Turn left at the stop sign half a block down, and keep walking."

"Thank you for the directions."

He stood up, and so did I. I was hoping that he would head for the door, but he didn't move. His next words were very measured. "You keep referring to these books. Please tell me why."

I sighed and glanced back at the waiting elevator. "Alexander Banks is a character in the Otherworld books." *As if you didn't know that.*

"And what role do I supposedly play in these books?"

"You're James's cousin. The vampire stalker."

He considered that. "I am aware of my actions being reported in the *Daily Sentinel*, but not in any books. Whatever these volumes say, I assure you they are entirely unauthorized. I am the real Alexander Banks. I give you my word."

"OK. You're Alexander Banks."

His nostrils flared. "You clearly do not believe me. How can I prove who I am?"

He probably expected me to quiz him on the books, but that wouldn't prove anything. If he was this much of a fan, he probably knew them even better than I did.

And then something occurred to me. I could end this, here and now.

"You could stick out your tongue."

"I beg your pardon?"

"Alexander Banks can't drink anything too sweet or tart because his tongue got slashed by a vampire's blade. If you show me the scar on your tongue, I'll believe you."

"Very well." He stuck out his tongue.

I gasped. There it was: a deep scar down the bottom half of his tongue. I was speechless.

He wasn't supposed to be able to prove that he was Alexander. What was I supposed to do now? Believe him?

He didn't stop there. "I have several other scars that may reinforce the verdict." He pushed back his coat and unbuttoned his shirt to reveal a circular white scar beneath his collarbone. I felt myself blush, despite my fear and frustration.

"James and I were nine, fencing with tree branches. He impaled me. I almost bled to death."

I nodded dumbly. The story was in *Otherworld*. It had been a terrifying experience for both boys, but it had brought them closer, making them more like brothers than cousins.

He began to roll up one of his sleeves. His forearm was muscular, and that made me blush, too. "I also have—"

"It's OK. I – I believe you."

The world was shifting around me. What choice did I have but to believe his wild story? It could be that he was crazy enough to mutilate himself in order to be Alexander. But the scars looked too old for him to have made them since the books came out.

Did that really mean, then. . . ?

Was this guy actually. . . ?

I closed my eyes for a second, trying to take it all in. When I opened them, Alexander was still there, life-size and three-dimensional. Despite the wariness in his eyes, he looked slightly younger than I'd pictured him. He was, after all, only a couple of months shy of nineteen.

"I just don't understand," I said. "How could you *be* the Alexander Banks from the books?"

"I have absolutely no idea. Which is why I must see these books you speak of. But first, please, tell me where I am. I know this city as well as I know the lines in my own palm, but I must have chased Vigo further than I thought."

Vigo.

No. No way. Vigo could not be here. He could not have attacked me.

But then I had a flash of memory of silver-blond hair and a low growling. I shivered violently.

"Are you well, miss?"

"Not if you're saying the guy who jumped me was actually Vigo."

"Indeed, it was."

I couldn't tell who was more confused right now, me or Alexander. "OK. I have to show you. The books, I mean. I think you'd better come up to my apartment . . . Alexander."

Saying his name was so strange. I'd said it so many times before, thought it more times than I could count. But I'd never expected I would say it to his face. In my dazed mind, it struck me that my greatest dream had come true: Alexander Banks was here. In my Chicago.

But so had my worst nightmare: Vigo was, too.

"Mom, this is my friend, Alexander. Alexander, Mom." I'd never imagined that Alexander Banks would be the first boy I brought home, but here he was in my living room.

Mom looked at me, then at Alexander, then at me. It didn't take a psychic to read her mind. *Who is he and why are you bringing him over at eleven thirty at night?*

"Nice to meet you, Alexander." She managed a smile, and self-consciously touched her hair, which was pulled back in an untidy ponytail. I could tell she was embarrassed to be meeting a guest in her Friday night sweats.

"Likewise." He didn't bow; I'd told him not to on the elevator ride up. I'd also told him to let me do all the talking.

"I'm going to get us something to eat, OK, Mom?"

"There's leftover shepherd's pie in the fridge. It's at the back. Here, I'll show you."

"Have a seat," I told Alexander. He sat down on the couch, riveted by the TV, which was playing a sitcom. He glanced at me with an astonished expression, but I shook my head. The last thing I needed was for my mom to hear him ask what a TV was.

In the kitchen, Mom looked at me expectantly.

"He's Luisa's brother's friend," I said, turning on the faucet and pouring two glasses of water. I hated lying to my mom, and preferred not to look her in the eye while I was doing it. "He needs a place to stay. I haven't asked him yet, but I was wondering if he could stay here for a couple of days."

"How come I haven't heard about him?"

I shrugged. "There was nothing to say. We weren't that close or anything. Where's the shepherd's pie?"

"Right here." She bent into the fridge and removed a glass dish covered in tinfoil. "Are you dating him?"

"No, it's not like that," I said quickly. "We're just friends."

A knowing look flickered in Mom's eyes. She could tell already that I had a crush on him. I waited for her to ask me flat out, but instead she said, "What about his parents?"

"They passed away a few years ago. He was living with his aunt, but they weren't getting along."

I was relieved to be able to tell the truth about that, at least. Alexander had lived with James's parents since he was orphaned. His aunt Helen had been troubled by Alexander's quest for vengeance, and when she persisted in trying to get him to abandon it, he cut her out of his life. She had passed away in *The Mists*, heartbroken that she couldn't turn him around.

"Why's he dressed like that?"

"He's an Otherworld fan, too. Some people at the dance were dressing up."

She smiled. "A boy who's an Otherworld fan? I'm sure you have a lot in common."

"Pretty much."

"I'll trust your judgement on this, Amy. He can stay for a couple of days."

"Thanks." I hugged her.

Mom always trusted my judgement; I'd never given her any reason not to. Unlike Chrissy, *I* was always responsible, reliable, and honest — until tonight, anyway. But I couldn't possibly tell her the truth about Alexander. If I did, she'd send both of us for mental evaluations.

I warmed the shepherd's pie in the microwave and brought it to Alexander along with a glass of water. He downed them fast. Mom said goodnight and headed off down the hall, then poked her head in a minute later to remind me to get clean sheets and towels for our guest.

Once she left again, Alexander looked at me. "Shall I take that for an offer of hospitality?"

"My mom said you could stay for a couple of days. I didn't tell her who you really are."

"I'd have thought my reputation would recommend me. If she reads the *Daily Sentinel*, she might well have heard of me."

"There is no *Daily Sentinel* here."

His brows furrowed. "Are we not in Chicago?"

"We're in Chicago, just not *your* Chicago. I don't know how, but you're not in Otherworld any more."

"What is Otherworld?"

I hesitated. "It's the place in the books. What I'm saying is, you're not in *your* world any more."

He appeared to mull this over. "Then where am I?"

"I don't know. *Here.*" I wished I could make him understand it, but I didn't understand it myself. "A place without vampires."

"You must be mistaken. You were clearly attacked by—"

"I know. But I don't know how he got here, or how you got here. Hold on a second. Let me get the books for you."

I went to my bedroom, scooped them off my bedside table, and brought them back.

He took both hardcovers into his hands, staring at the pictures on the book jackets. "Good heavens, that's me! And James! And *her.*" Alexander had always been dead set against James's relationship with Hannah. He didn't believe humans and vampires should mix, much less fall in love.

He opened *Otherworld*, flipping through the pages. I sat down beside him, making sure we weren't sitting too close together. Then I showed him a section midway through the book that took place from his point of view.

"Astounding," he muttered.

He studied the books for a while, occasionally making a shocked exclamation. And *I* studied him in a daze, trying to make sense of the fact that Alexander Banks was here beside me. In my *living room*. On my *couch*. I thought about touching him to make sure he was real, but I wouldn't dare. Just the thought made my face flame.

Could this be a trick of some kind, an elaborate hoax set up to dupe an Otherworld fan for a reality TV show? I could see Luisa and Katie nominating me for something like that. Maybe there were hidden cameras outside, and even here in the apartment. I glanced around, seeing nothing out of the ordinary.

Besides, the attack had been too violent to have been staged. Any producers would know that I could've got seriously hurt and sued the pants off them. And my mom would never have played along with a stunt like that.

My gut said that Alexander was the real thing. I would just have to trust my instincts – until I had evidence to prove otherwise.

Eventually, Alexander put the books aside and sank back into the couch, raking a hand through his dark hair. "I don't know what to make of it."

"I don't, either. Maybe you chased Vigo through a portal of some kind."

"A portal? In my world, portals are the stuff of fiction."

"Here, too. But there must be some reason that you started off chasing Vigo in Otherworld Chicago, and you ended up chasing him here in the real Chicago."

The moment I saw his face twitch, I wished I could take back the words.

"You believe that *my* world is the fantasy world, do you?" Alexander asked. "I assure you, it is not. *This* world, which you claim has no vampires and has oddities such as" – he glanced at the TV – "miniature film projectors, seems fantastical to me."

I didn't know how to respond. In a way, he was right — his world was completely real to him. Alexander Banks was not, and never had been, a fictional character.

My first thought was that I had to call Katie and Luisa, tell them everything. But I knew how crazy the whole scenario would sound. I'd have to wait.

"I'm sorry," I finally said. "I didn't mean that. Your world is as real as mine."

"Thank you." He seemed deep in thought. "There must be some passageway between my Chicago and yours. Otherwise, this author could not have known what is happening there." He paused. "If a portal exists, I believe it is located in the vicinity of the Michigan Avenue Bridge. Earlier this evening, I tracked down Vigo and chased him across the bridge. Soon after, I became aware that I did not recognize where we were. I didn't understand it because the bridge ends off in the Elgin District, and we clearly weren't there. Come to think of it, that's when I noticed that many people were out past curfew."

"And then you ended up at my building complex."

"Yes. I'd lost Vigo's trail briefly. I imagine that he was as disoriented as I was. That must be why he stopped to feed — he didn't appear to realize that I was still after him."

Stopped to feed. I felt queasy. If Alexander hadn't shown up, Vigo would have. . . I shook my head. There was no time for post-traumatic stress disorder. We had to figure out what was happening.

"Maybe if you go back to the bridge," I suggested, "there's a chance you'll find your way home." I wasn't sure if that would work; after all, I'd crossed that bridge many times myself and never ended up in Otherworld. But it might be worth a shot.

"Getting home is not my primary concern." He gave me a hard glance, and I knew what was he was thinking. Any Alexander fan would know.

"You want to find Vigo."

"Until I know for certain that Vigo has returned to my world, I'm not going anywhere."

$\mathcal{F}$our

Last night. The attack. *Alexander.*

Had I dreamed it all? Or was Alexander, right now, sleeping on the lumpy pullout couch in the den?

I shifted to look at the clock, wincing at the soreness all over my body. Pushing the covers back, I saw bruises on my arms where Vigo had grabbed me. It was all the assurance I needed that last night had really happened.

7:39 a.m. My second Saturday waking up way too early. But there was no chance of falling back to sleep. I was surprised I'd slept at all, since I'd lain awake for hours, my mind spinning.

I opted for jeans and a knit top, slowly pulling the clothes over my sore body. After brushing my teeth, I went back to my room to put on lipgloss and brush my hair. I glanced around. As always, my room was messy, spilling over with books. A sign hung on my door: Creative minds are seldom tidy. Still, I threw the scattered socks and T-shirts into my hamper.

What was I doing? A guy from Otherworld would never enter a girl's bedroom. It would ruin their reputations.

My face got hot.

The apartment was quiet. Mom and Chrissy were still asleep – they both liked to sleep in on Saturdays. I peeked in the den, and saw that the sheets and pillow were still stacked on the couch. I heard some noise in the kitchen, so I headed that way.

And there was Alexander, sitting at the kitchen table with a cup of tea, engrossed in *Otherworld*.

He raised his eyes. "Good morning, Amy."

Hearing my name spoken in his soft, deep voice was startling.

"Did you sleep well?" I asked, trying to compose myself.

"I have not slept yet. I went out hoping to regain his trail. Then, at dawn, I returned and started reading. I hope you do not mind that I used your keys."

"It's OK." I spotted the keys on the table by the front door, where I'd left them. I should have known that Alexander would be keeping vampire time. It made sense, if you were a vampire hunter. I hadn't heard him leave or come back, but stealth had always been one of his strong points.

"I sleep in the afternoons," Alexander explained. "But then, I suppose you know that. I suppose you know a lot about me." His mouth tightened. "It seems there is no detail of my life too minute for Elizabeth Howard to share with the world."

I managed a smile. "That's what makes Otherworld so fascinating. The details."

"I am sure she would be glad of your approval."

"Where did you go last night?"

"All over this city of yours. It is a funny thing. Some streets go by the same names as in my Chicago, others are different. Some areas I recognize, others have changed irrevocably. I will have to study maps before going out again tonight." With that, he turned his attention back to the book.

I saw a plate with bread crumbs and the butter dish in front of him. Last night, I'd told him to help himself to food in the morning, but I wasn't sure bread and butter would do the trick. "I'll make us some eggs."

"Do not trouble yourself. I have had my sustenance."

"I'll make them, anyway." I felt like I needed a more substantial than usual breakfast myself.

Deciding scrambled eggs with salsa and cheese was the way to go, I put a pan on the stove and got the ingredients from the fridge. I was no gourmet chef, but I'd done a lot of cooking. With Mom having so many irregular shifts while I was growing up, she often wasn't home at dinnertime, and Dad could've happily had us live on hot dogs and baked beans.

I darted a glance over my shoulder.

Alexander Banks is in my kitchen.

It was going to take some getting used to.

The sleeves of his white shirt were rolled up, and his long legs were stretched out in front of him, hugged by old-fashioned brown trousers. He was beautiful, more so than I had ever imagined.

I tried to put the thought out of my head. Fantasizing about a fictional guy was one thing: fantasizing about him when he was sitting a few feet away was another. He'd quickly figure me out if I kept staring at him this way.

When the eggs were done, I divided them onto two plates, placing one in front of him.

"Thank you. It is very kind of you."

"You're welcome." I knew he'd probably feel obligated to ask me to join him, but I didn't want to stop him from reading, so I said, "I'm going to eat in the other room so you can read." Before he could argue, I went into the living room.

Sitting down on the couch, I turned on a local station. A puffy-eyed reporter was at a crime scene. Yellow tape blocked off a park behind him. "Two teenage boys were found dead on a basketball court in Archer Park, apparently with teeth-marks on their necks. The police are being tight-lipped about this, Jane, but I think they're flabbergasted. We've never seen anything like it."

Oh, God.

I put my face in my hands. This couldn't really be happening, could it? Vigo on a rampage in my city?

And I'd almost been his victim. My gut twisted. I bet he'd killed those poor guys after Alexander had foiled his attack on me.

I hadn't called the police last night. Maybe I should have.

Would they have put out some sort of notice? Would it have stopped two teenage guys from playing late-night basketball?

The couch dipped beside me as Alexander sat down, his dark gaze riveted on the TV. "Is this happening at the present time?"

I nodded.

I saw the knife-thin crease between his brows as he listened to the news of the murders. If I'd had any doubt that Alexander was who he said he was, or that my attacker last night had been Vigo, I didn't any more.

Alexander had been so close to catching Vigo at the end of *The Mists* that he'd had readers jumping out of their seats. But would he be able to get that close to him again in a city he didn't know?

"I am going to need excellent maps of the city," Alexander said, his eyes not straying from the TV. "Schematics of underground tunnels and sewer systems are essential."

"Don't you think you should take a couple of days to get to know the city?" I asked. "If you don't know your way around, it could work against you."

"Vigo doesn't know the city, either. He would not have his usual hiding places, nor the protection of his coven." He took a breath. "This could be the chance I've been waiting for."

Alexander had a point. And though I was afraid for his safety, I was also afraid for everyone else in this city. They didn't know there was a real vampire around.

"I'll get you maps. And some clothes, too. So you won't attract attention."

"I appreciate your help and hospitality." He turned to me, a chilling resolve in his eyes. "Let me assure you that I will do everything in my power to stop Vigo before he can cause more terror. I do not wish your world to become like mine."

Me neither.

An hour later, Alexander Banks walked into the mall wearing my Cubs jersey, his own trousers, and high leather boots. The odd fashion got him some stares, and I was eager to get him into other clothes. But the unusual getup didn't make him any less handsome, and I could tell that many of the stares were from intrigued females.

As Alexander and I headed towards the big department store at the south end of the mall, I glanced around, hoping we wouldn't bump into anyone I knew from school. Thankfully, Katie and Luisa were both busy with family obligations that day. And it was just after nine o'clock and the mall was half empty. But I was still paranoid.

Alexander, too, was looking around, but his eyes were wide and he seemed almost overwhelmed.

"This is definitely not my Chicago," he said. "I have never seen anything like this. So many lights and colours. It is dizzying."

"Are there shopping malls where you're from?" I couldn't remember one being mentioned in the books.

"There are shopping plazas of various kinds. None as colossal as this one. And all of them are aglow with natural light, for obvious reasons." He looked upward towards the huge skylight. "Are there parts of this plaza that are not exposed to natural light?"

"I think so. There are lots of stores in the basement."

Alexander's gaze grew troubled. "Then he can move about here by day, if he likes."

The thought made me shudder. Even though we were on the ground level with plenty of natural light, I found myself glancing over my shoulder. "There are a lot of places where he could move around in the daytime. Malls, cinemas, office buildings. And there are miles of underground subway tunnels all over the city."

Alexander nodded, looking determined. "Let us get this shopping done, Amy, so I can study the schematics."

When we arrived at the department store, Alexander glanced around in amazement again. "Such a vast selection of . . . everything," he said, taking in the aisles of goods. "How does one choose?"

I showed him some track pants on a reduced rack, which he said looked ridiculous. I guess people didn't wear track pants in Otherworld Chicago. But when I told him they were for sports, he seemed open to trying them on. I offered him some khakis, which he approved of. Then he picked up some T-shirts, a sweatshirt, a jacket, socks, and some toiletries.

"I will find a way to repay you," he said later as we walked out of the store with our purchases. I knew that it was hard for him to let me buy these things, but he had no choice. Until he got to know my world better, he would have to rely on me.

"You saved my life, and you're trying to protect my city. It's the least I can do," I said truthfully.

"I am, nonetheless, grateful." He rubbed his temple, as if the lights were giving him a headache. "Are we done here?"

"One more thing. I think you should have some running shoes." I eyed his battered leather boots.

"My boots are adequate."

"Maybe, but take a look at these." I turned into an athletic store, leading him to the sneaker section, where dozens of options were displayed on the walls.

Alexander picked up a Nike cross trainer. "Strange design."

"Why don't you try it? It might be easier to run in these than your boots."

"This shoe clearly is not my size, and there is no time to have more made."

I tried not to laugh. "They have some in the back room that are your size," I explained. It was funny, the things we took for granted in our daily lives.

A salesperson came up, asking if he wanted to try them on.

"He'll try them on, but he's not sure of his size," I answered for him. "Could you measure his feet?"

Alexander submitted to having his feet measured, then waited in his socks for the salesman to bring the sneakers. He put them on and walked a few steps. "These won't do at all. They feel as though I am walking on marshmallows. Thank you, Amy, but my boots will do just fine."

Again, I bit back my laughter. "They're called *running* shoes. They should help you run even faster than you do now."

"Faster?" That got his attention. He jumped up and down several times to test out the sneakers. "I will take them."

I wasn't keen on the hundred-dollar price tag, but anything that could help Alexander catch up with Vigo would be worth it.

Alexander changed into the new clothes in the mall bathroom. When we got home, it was eleven thirty. Luckily, Chrissy still wasn't up, and Mom had left a note to say she'd gone out for groceries, which could take a while. I did a quick Internet search and downloaded as many maps of the city as I could find, then printed them all. Alexander laid them out on the kitchen table and studied them, asking me questions as he did. He wanted me to describe different parts of the city, landmarks, topography, everything. I thought I knew my city well, but I wasn't able to give him all the details he wanted. I did, however, go back to the Internet several times to look things up for him.

At one point, Chrissy appeared in the doorway of the kitchen, sleep-rumpled, in a short nightgown. "Who's *that*?" she asked, looking over at Alexander.

It wasn't that Chrissy had never learned manners, I thought irritably; she just didn't use them.

"This is my friend Alexander. He's staying with us for a couple of days."

"Staying here? Why?"

Alexander looked up from the maps, his glare cool. "And who are you?"

She seemed taken aback. "Chrissy."

"Chrissy?" he repeated, as though it didn't sound right. "It is not a name I am familiar with."

"It's short for Christina," I explained.

"I see," he said with a nod. "That is a name I recognize, to be sure."

"Do you have a problem with my name or something?" Chrissy asked suspiciously.

"No." He looked puzzled. "Do you?" When she didn't immediately reply, he turned his attention back to the maps, effectively shutting her down.

Chrissy made a face, then grabbed a box of Pop-Tarts and retreated. I followed her into the living room.

"Who is that guy?" she demanded. "And why does he have to stay *here*?"

"He's a friend of a friend and needed a place to stay. Please be nice to him." If Mom was going to support Alexander staying here, I needed Chrissy on our side, too.

"*I'm* always nice." She bit into a Pop-Tart. "*He* was totally rude."

"He didn't mean to be. You just caught him at a bad time. He works nights and hasn't gone to bed yet."

"He hasn't gone to bed yet? That's crazy. Where does he work?"

I thought fast. "An all-night convenience store downtown."

"A convenience store, seriously? Doesn't he go to school? He looks old enough to be in college."

Like Chrissy was one to judge. She didn't go to school as often as she was supposed to.

"I don't know what his plans are," I answered.

Chrissy shot me a glance. "He's cute, you know."

I chose to ignore that.

Chrissy plopped down on the sofa and turned on the TV. The local news was still reporting on the murdered teens.

Chrissy listened, mouth gaping open. "Did you see?" She turned to glare at me. "Some crazy person's out there killing people, pretending to be a vampire. It's 'cause of those vampire books you read."

"You don't know that," I shot back. If only Chrissy knew how closely tied to the books the murders were. "But anyway," I added, "we should all be extra careful. There's obviously someone dangerous on the loose."

"Scary." She said it lightly, but I could tell that the news had affected her. "I'm going to take a shower." She turned off the TV, and flounced out.

When I turned my head, Alexander was standing there. He had the maps rolled up in his hands like a scroll.

"Your sister is an interesting specimen." From his tone, I could tell it wasn't a compliment. Chrissy did have a way of rubbing people the wrong way.

"She's going through a phase. A *long* phase."

"Her manners are lacking. So unlike your own."

"Thanks," I said, hiding my smile. "Chrissy can get under people's skin. I try not to let it bother me."

"Are you successful?"

"Not always. She's been much worse since my father left."

"Your father left? Did he go to war?"

I almost laughed. "No, nothing that noble. He left one day after telling my mom he was seeing another woman."

Alexander whistled under his breath. "What he did is unthinkable. I know of few men who would do such a thing. Women and children should never be without a man to protect and provide for them."

I bristled, but then realized where Alexander was coming from – literally. "It's different here. We don't need a man's protection. A lot of men, and women, too, leave their families and start new ones. The whole *till death do us part* thing hasn't been true for a long time."

Alexander frowned. "It is a bitter pill to swallow."

"Yeah."

"Your father appears to be a cad of the first order."

I knew the word "cad" from the books. It meant jerk.

"He doesn't think he's done anything wrong. He says he didn't mean to fall in love with someone else. Anyway, there's no point in arguing with him. When I give him a hard time, I don't hear from him again for weeks." I was surprised at how natural it felt to confide in Alexander, as if I'd known him for ages.

"That is because of his guilt," Alexander said thoughtfully.

"Maybe. I wouldn't know."

"I *do* know, Amy. Because I have hurt people, and I've hated to look them in the eye."

I knew what he was talking about. "Aunt Helen."

"Yes. My one regret is the disappointment I caused her. She was a remarkable woman."

I bit my lip, wondering if he had read the scene in *The Mists* where Helen is on her deathbed. She tells James that she failed in raising Alexander because she had not been able to break his obsession with Vigo and help him build a life for himself. She died with that sadness.

I felt a lump in my throat. I'd cried when Helen passed away. You could feel her warmth and kindness radiating from the pages. Now that I knew Helen had been a real person, it was all the more sad.

"I hope it doesn't bother you that I know so much about your life," I said.

Alexander tilted his head to one side. "It irks me that this Elizabeth Howard person has shared so much without my permission. But I have no problem with you knowing. You have been nothing but generous and forthcoming with me. I am in your debt."

"No, you're not. I'm in yours."

"I will argue the point at another time. Right now, I should sleep."

"Of course." He needed to rest if he was going to hunt tonight. I quickly made up the pullout couch for him in the den, then shut the door to give him privacy.

As I went to my room, I wondered how Alexander would ever find Vigo. Though Vigo might not have his favourite hiding spots, he could easily find new ones. My Chicago offered more and better hiding places than the damp, dark cellars and sewers of Otherworld. Here, every major building had a finished basement with artificial lighting. Vigo could hide in comfort in thousands of locations across the city.

If only I could warn the public that the threat was far worse than they knew. Then it occurred to me that there was something I actually could do. I had a description of the killer, didn't I? I could call Crime Stoppers.

I grabbed my cell phone and dialled.

"This is about the vampire murders."

"Go ahead," the female said in a nasal voice.

"I know what the murderer looks like. He attacked me last night, but I got away. He was acting like a vampire." As much as I wanted to tell her he was a *real* vampire, there was no way she'd believe me. "He even wears fangs."

"You say he attacked you, ma'am?"

"Yes."

"We'd like you to come in and talk to the police immediately."

"I can't. I'm . . . too scared." I heard my voice waver with real fear. "I'll tell you what he looks like. That's all I can do. He has silvery blond hair." I remembered his description vividly from the books. "He has light blue eyes and really pale skin. Average height, I think. He's really strong, but you can't tell by looking at him. He's very lean."

"Thank you, ma'am. I hope you'll reconsider coming in and speaking to investigators. I can guarantee your anonymity. It sounds like you have enough information to be helpful to them."

"Please, just pass on this information."

"I will, but we've already got hundreds of tips on this case, and by the end of the day, we might have thousands. If you don't feel comfortable speaking to investigators, can you give me more corroborating evidence? In what part of the city did he attack you?"

"The east side. Near Pleasant Park."

"When was this?"

"Friday night."

"What time?"

"Around eleven."

"OK, ma'am. Thank you for calling Crime Stoppers."

I snapped the phone shut, taking a deep breath. She probably hadn't believed a word I'd said. Hundreds of people were likely calling in descriptions of the odd loner down the street or jerk ex-boyfriends.

I felt powerless. I hoped Alexander could catch Vigo, because if he didn't, the city had no idea what it was in for.

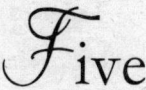

Five

Soundless, voiceless nightmares rolled from one scenario to another. In the worst one, vampires crowded on the fire escape outside my window, begging me to let them in. And I decided to open the window to talk peace. That's when they pounced, of course.

I hated when I was stupid in dreams.

Sunday morning. I woke up from a fitful sleep – the type of sleep where I wasn't sure I'd slept at all. How could I relax knowing Alexander was out there and in danger?

I'd seen him only briefly last night. He'd woken up just before sunset, eaten the leftover casserole Mom had made, then went out into the night. When Mom looked at me questioningly, I told her the same story I'd told Chrissy about his job at the all-night convenience store.

I felt a wave of relief when I saw him on the living room couch. He must have finished *Otherworld* already, because he was reading *The Mists*.

"Hi," I said, smiling. He was so handsome it made my chest tighten.

His mouth curved into a smile that didn't reach his eyes. There was no need to ask how his night of hunting had gone. "Good morning."

I spotted a newspaper on the table next to him. The headline read: COINCIDENCE? It showed a picture of Friday night's crime scene alongside a picture of Elizabeth Howard.

"I found this outside your neighbour's apartment," he said, handing me the paper. "Astonishing story, isn't it? The Otherworld phenomenon is so great that the author is being criticized for somehow inciting the killings."

I sat down beside him and read the article. Chrissy had been right. People *were* connecting the release of The Mists with the vampire killings. Some were even calling for the Otherworld books to be banned.

"It is difficult to comprehend," he said.

I nodded. "Just because Elizabeth Howard writes about vampires doesn't mean she should be blamed for the killings."

"I meant the popularity of the series is difficult to understand. The better part of it is romantic drivel. James and Hannah as star-crossed lovers? It insults my sensibilities."

"It's different when you're looking in from the outside. People like melodrama and . . . romance."

"Melodrama and romance? Is that why people care about what's going on in my world?"

"That's part of it. Personally, your story line of avenging your family is the one I find most interesting, not James and Hannah's relationship."

He scowled. "What he possibly sees in her, I'll never know."

"Hey, I'd like to show you something. Come with me." I went to the den and pressed the button to boot up the computer, then gestured for him to sit down. I pulled up a chair for myself.

He gazed at the computer in fascination. "Is this similar to the one in the living room? With live news reports?"

"No, that's a TV. A computer is like. . ." How the heck did I explain a computer? "It's a machine that holds a lot of information. Almost anything you'd find in a library or newspaper is on here. And it's also like a typewriter, except you can see the words on the screen instead of on paper."

"Extraordinary," he muttered, glancing behind the monitor, as if looking for a projector of some kind.

I typed my log-in and my screen came up. The desktop background was a picture of the cover of *The Mists of Otherworld*.

He looked at me. "Do all of these computer machines have this picture on them?"

"No, I put it there myself. You can put whatever picture you want on your computer."

"I see."

I reached past him to open a web browser, and my arm accidentally brushed his. Just that bit of contact sent a warm ripple through me. I heard my heart beating in my ears, probably because I was holding my breath.

My home page was *Otherworlders*, one of the top fan communities. I liked it not only because it had all the latest news about the series, but because it had a fan fiction forum.

Alexander was fascinated. "So you're saying that when someone else puts on a computer, this is not what appears on their screen."

"Right. When my sister opens it, she's at the home page of Metal Mouth, her favourite band. Now, look at this." I logged on to the main Otherworlder forum.

He looked closely at the screen, glancing from side to side. "What is all this?"

"It's people talking about the books." I used the mouse to click on the latest post. "Someone here wanted to talk about the ending of *The Mists*, and almost four hundred people responded in the last few hours."

"Remarkable. Wait a minute – who is Mrs Alexander Banks eight thousand and twenty-one?"

Uh-oh. He'd spotted the small icon at the top with my log-in name. I felt my face heat up. "It's just, uh, a name. Everyone has to log in under a made-up name."

He turned to me, narrowing his eyes. "Is this *your* made-up name?"

I wished he'd stop looking at me. I knew I was bright red. "Yes, but it's just a joke. I mean, there are thousands of other Mrs

Alexander Bankses. That's why I'm number eight thousand and twenty-one."

"Hmm." He seemed puzzled by the whole thing. "I am glad, at least, to see that some readers support my cause. Wait a minute." He pressed his finger against the screen. "Is that person claiming to be Vigo's lover?"

He'd spotted a username called *VigosVampLover*.

"It's just a joke, I told you. She doesn't know Vigo is real."

"Joke or not, it isn't funny."

"Let me show you something else," I suggested. "It's called email. Electronic mail. You can send a letter through the computer."

After I showed him how to send an email, I showed him how to check the weather, the local news, the times of sunrise and sunset. With every new page, his face lit up like a kid on Christmas. He asked question after question, until finally he pushed back from the computer.

"I would love to bring this knowledge back to my world. When the vampires came, almost a hundred years ago, many of our brightest minds fled. Anyone with money fled. It is no wonder we are stuck in the past." He looked saddened. Then he picked up *The Mists*, which he'd brought with him to the computer. "I can't believe how many people have read these books." He flipped to the author photo on the inside back cover, a glamorous shot of Elizabeth Howard. "It is essential that I speak to the author. Perhaps I could speak to her on the telephone, or we could arrange to meet."

Contacting the author — of course! It made sense; she might be the only person able to explain how it was possible that Alexander and Vigo existed, and had come to our world. But how would we do it? "It's not easy to get in touch with someone as famous as her," I told him. "I'm sure her address and phone number would be unlisted."

"We must find a way. She may have some insight into finding Vigo. Perhaps she knows where he is right now. And I need to understand how she could possibly know so many details of my life — including my thoughts."

"Maybe," I said, my mind racing, "Elizabeth Howard goes through the same portal that you and Vigo came through, and that's why she knows Otherworld so well. But that doesn't explain how she'd know her characters' thoughts."

"However she does it, it's totally objectionable. And I intend to tell her so after she has helped me locate Vigo."

"I'll check her tour dates. I know she isn't coming to Chicago until November, but she might be someplace else we can get to." I turned back to the computer. It took me less than a minute to find the information. "She'll be signing in New York City next weekend. That's a long way, but it's manageable. We could take a bus."

Alexander nodded. "New York City it is. I am most eager to make Elizabeth Howard's acquaintance."

"Can we talk?" Mom poked her head into my bedroom that night, knocking a tune on the door.

"Sure." I had been trying to do homework for tomorrow, but wasn't getting anywhere.

Mom came in and sat on my bed. "It's about Alexander."

I could tell she was searching for words, so I jumped in. "I know you said a couple of days, but I was hoping he could stay a bit longer. Please, Mom. He's not any trouble, is he?"

She sighed. "Not to me. But Chrissy isn't comfortable having a boy around."

"I don't buy it, Mom. She hasn't even given him a chance." I wasn't comfortable with Madison around, but I put up with *her*.

"I know how Chrissy can be," she said in a whisper. "But that isn't the issue. I'm concerned that Alexander needs to figure his life out right now, and we're not helping him by letting him stay here. He sleeps all day and goes out all night. Then he gets up, eats, and is off again."

"I told you, that's because he works nights and is saving up money. It's not like he's out partying."

Mom nodded, but still looked dubious.

"He's extremely hardworking." That part, at least, was true. "He'll pay you back anything you spend on groceries."

She shook her head. "I'm not concerned about that. I'm more concerned about *you* – that he's taking advantage of your kindness."

I couldn't blame her for coming to that conclusion. "He's not manipulating us, Mom. He's just in a rough spot right now. I wish you could understand."

"Would it help if I talked to his aunt for him? Maybe I could help them patch things up?"

"It's too late for that. Could he stay just a few more days? I'll help him look for a room to rent."

"Does he have money to pay for a room?"

"He has some." I had about five hundred and fifty dollars, I thought, remembering the bank statement from the ATM the other day. But it wouldn't stretch very far if it had to cover rent and food.

She patted my hand. "I'll take a look at the bulletin board at the hospital to see if there are any rooms for rent."

"Thanks, Mom."

When she left, I curled my fists in frustration. Not only did Alexander have to worry about hunting Vigo, he'd soon be homeless if I didn't find him somewhere to stay.

If Mom only knew what Alexander had done for me Friday night, she'd probably let him move in for ever. But I couldn't tell Mom — she'd be horrified if she knew I'd been attacked, even if she didn't know it was by a vampire. And I couldn't see any reason to put her through that.

I got up from the bed and went to look out the window. The sun had set, and darkness blanketed the streets except for the glow of streetlights. Alexander was out there looking for Vigo. I wished I could do something, anything, to help him. But here, like in Otherworld, he chose to hunt alone.

$\mathcal{S}$ix

MONDAY MORNING PASSED BY in a blur of classes and endless talk about the vampire killer. Everyone was freaked out that the two boys had been killed, but I kept silent, not wanting to reveal to anyone what I knew. I hadn't seen Alexander in the apartment that morning, but I had a feeling he would have let me know somehow if he had caught Vigo.

At lunchtime, I met up with Luisa and Katie in the cafeteria line. On today's menu: noodles in a lumpy, ketchuplike sauce. Although lunch only cost two bucks, I was beginning to think we were being overcharged.

We snagged our usual spot at one end of a long folding table. Like everyone else at school, all Katie and Luisa wanted to talk about was the vampire killings. I was quiet, wrestling over whether or not I should tell my best friends about Alexander. On the one hand, I felt like I *had* to — I confided in the girls about everything, and this was huge, life altering. On the other hand, I knew Alexander wanted to fly under the radar as much as possible. If I told anyone the truth about him, there was a chance word would spread and Alexander's presence here would get out.

"Usually there's safety in numbers," Luisa said as she twirled the noodles around her fork. "Not any more. This guy somehow managed to attack two people at once." the noodles around her fork. "Not any more. This guy somehow managed to attack two people at once."

Katie looked doubtful. "It can't be just one person. Nobody's that strong."

No human, anyway. I flashed back to Friday night, felt the panic rise inside me, and squelched it.

"We should all stay inside after dark until this guy is caught," I cautioned them.

Katie lifted her chin. "I'm not letting this wannabe vampire punk change how I live my life. Then he wins."

"It's not admitting defeat if people lay low for a while," I argued. "It's being smart. If we go out at night, we should all take cabs."

"I can't afford to do that for more than a week," Katie said. Her family's money situation was similar to mine. They got by on her mom's salary as a bank cashier, but there wasn't a lot left over. Still, Katie had a sweet summer job as a camp counselor and usually came home with at least two grand in the bank.

"Amy?"

I turned to see Mrs Benedetti, the office administrator,

standing behind me. She looked peeved. "There's a young man in the office asking to see you. He says his name is Alexander and that he's your fiancé. He's extremely insistent."

Alexander was *here*? And what was he thinking, calling himself my fiancé?

Luisa gasped. "Fiancé?"

"Amy – what the—" Katie stammered.

Mrs Benedetti cut them off before they could ask any coherent questions. "Well?" she said to me. "Do you know who this person is, or should we call the police?"

"I know him." I shot Katie and Luisa an *I'll explain later* look, then stood up and left the cafeteria.

I followed Mrs Benedetti down the hall towards the office. Alexander's voice reached me before I got there.

". . . and I assure you, madam, that she will be quite happy to see me," he said sharply.

"Yes, but since she's under eighteen and you're not her parent, we can't let you speak to her without her permission," replied Mrs Pearsen, the office administrative assistant.

In the doorway, I said, "Hi, um, honey."

Alexander turned to me, a satisfied look on his face, then glanced back at Mrs Pearsen. "As you can see, my fiancée is delighted I am here."

Mrs Pearsen gave me a stern look, as if to say that the fiancée charade was not amusing. But mostly, she seemed relieved to have him off her back. "You need to wear this as long as you're in the building. School policy." She handed him a visitor's pass.

He took it and we left the office together. Since everyone was either in the lunchroom or in class, the halls were deserted.

"Try to be more polite next time, Alexander," I whispered. "I thought you didn't want to attract attention." I noticed he was wearing one of the new T-shirts and the khakis we had bought together. At least he blended in. He carried a plastic grocery bag that appeared to contain a book.

"I was extremely polite."

"Well, in this world, you should try to tone it down. We don't use aggression to get what we want." I paused, realizing that wasn't true for a lot of people. But still, it was true for me, and he was dragging me into this. "You shouldn't have told them you were my fiancé."

"I thought if I were your fiancé, they would let me see you immediately."

"It just made you sound weird. Nobody my age gets married."

"But you're, what, sixteen? Seventeen?"

"Seventeen in January. Way too young to get married. Or even engaged."

And if I should be married at sixteen . . . why aren't you married already? I thought. Then I remembered that Alexander had devoted his life to hunting vampires. That didn't leave a lot of time for romance.

"Obviously I have much to learn about your world," Alexander replied. "Forgive my intrusion – I tried to reach you by telephone, but yours appeared to be malfunctioning. I kept hearing your voice telling me to leave a message, with strange music in the background."

"That's my voice mail. I'm not allowed to have my phone turned on at school. If they catch us on the phone, they'll take it away. Next time borrow someone's cell phone and send me a text message."

"What is a text message?"

"I'll show you another time. Let's see if we can find a private study room in the library. I know the librarian, so please be nice to her. Just follow my lead, OK?"

Ms P was perched on a stool behind the checkout desk. When she saw me, her eyes brightened. When she saw Alexander, she couldn't hide her surprise.

Was it so surprising that I'd be with a hot guy? Yes, I suppose it was. And Alexander was the kind of hot that simply didn't exist in this dimension.

"Hey, Ms P. This is my friend Alexander."

"Enchanted, madam." Alexander gave a little bow.

Ms P seemed startled, but charmed, too. "Nice to meet you, Alexander."

"Is there a study room free where we can hang out for a while?" I asked.

Ms P frowned slightly, and I hoped she didn't think we wanted a private place to make out. Not that that would be a bad thing.

"The room at the end is free," she said.

We headed to the study room at the end of the hall. Each room had several computers; sometimes classes came here to do research or to get a library lesson. At lunchtime, students could book these rooms to work on projects or have club meetings.

I closed the door behind us, glad that we had privacy to talk. One of the walls was a window, so we could be seen by anyone who came to this end of the hall, but we couldn't be heard. We sat down across from each other at the centre table.

There were shadows under his eyes. I could tell he hadn't slept yet.

"You should go to bed, Alexander."

"I will, do not worry. I came to tell you that I have finished reading *The Mists of Otherworld* and have made a stunning discovery."

"What is it?"

He leaned closer to me. "In the first book, Elizabeth Howard writes only one short section from Vigo's perspective, but in *The Mists of Otherworld*, she writes several. And in doing so, she has revealed something that could help me catch him." He took the hardcover from the bag and opened it to page 374. I skimmed the page, then looked up at him, eyes wide.

"Vigo's equation of probabilities. You didn't know about it?" I asked, surprised.

"No. I don't think anyone in my world knows about it. All of these years I wondered what his strategy was for eluding me. I knew that he had received an education in mathematics when he was mortal, but I never realized he could use a mathematical formula to evade capture. Now that I know his theory, it may give me the upper hand."

I could've kicked myself. It hadn't occurred to me that there might be information in the books that Alexander *didn't* know. I wondered, for the thousandth time, how it was possible that Elizabeth Howard knew the thoughts of the people in Otherworld.

"That's amazing, but what if Vigo knows about the books already?" I asked. "He's been here as long as you have, and might have seen an ad in a bookstore window. If he knows his formula is in the book, he might not use it again. Or he might change it."

Alexander nodded. "That is a distinct possibility. But knowing that he uses any formula at all helps me to understand how he thinks, and that may be the key. Now, if Vigo knows about the books, we have a more pressing problem on our hands: he knows about Elizabeth Howard."

My gut tightened. "You think he'll go after her?"

"He might. If Vigo is furious enough, there is no telling what he might do."

"But why would he be furious with her? Vigo likes attention. Maybe he'll love the idea of being famous in two worlds."

"Howard's portrayal would infuriate him for other reasons," he said. "She has not only revealed his probabilities equation, she has aired all of his insecurities. She has described in detail, for instance, how little he trusts Leander, the second-in-command of his coven. And she revealed something that would make him angriest of all." He smiled. "She revealed that he fears me." He flipped to page 421.

> *"He's here? Alexander is here?" Vigo didn't want to admit, even to himself, the cold feeling that gnawed at him. It was one he was not accustomed to, and it was one he despised himself for having.*
>
> *He rather thought it was fear.*

I looked up from the page, my mind racing. "We have to warn Elizabeth Howard."

"Yes."

"I just hope she'll listen to us."

"Take heart, Amy. I have every confidence that—"

His gaze flickered to the window. Katie and Luisa stood outside the room, giggling.

I motioned for them to come in.

"Are you going to introduce us to your *fiancé*?" Katie asked as they walked in.

Alexander got out of his chair and bowed.

Their eyebrows went up.

"I'm Katie." She shook his hand.

Luisa did, too. "Luisa."

"Delighted."

There was a tense silence.

Finally Katie said, "So how do you guys know each other?"

My mouth opened, but nothing came out. I hadn't expected Alexander to show up at school, so I hadn't thought up an explanation.

"We met in the park over the weekend," Alexander said smoothly, "while I was taking a stroll."

I knew he was trying to help, but I wished he wouldn't. Maybe meeting on a stroll in the park was common in Otherworld, but not here.

"Oh, yeah?" Luisa grinned. "Is that when you got engaged?"

Before Alexander could say something weird, I answered, "Alexander has a quirky sense of humour. The office staff didn't get the joke." I turned to him. "Thanks for stopping by. It was good to see you."

"And you." Taking the hint, he inclined his head to my friends, and left.

They held their hands over their mouths until he was out of range, then burst out laughing.

"What was *that* about, Ames?" Luisa cried. "You didn't tell me you met a guy! He's gorgeous – total Alexander Banks look-alike! How old is he?"

"Eighteen." And would be nineteen on the second of December, I didn't add. "I'm not dating him. We're getting to know each other as friends."

Katie frowned. "You've gotta be careful. Did he really just

come up to you in the park?"

"No, he was just joking about that." The lie jumped into my head a second later. "He's a friend of my cousin, Dave."

"Oh, cool," Katie said. "It's strange that he's already stopping by your school, though, isn't it? Maybe he's a stalker."

Luisa snorted. "A guy that good-looking can't be a stalker. Girls should be stalking *him*. It's neat that his name's Alexander, don't you think? Just like Alexander Banks? Maybe it's *destiny*."

Fortunately, the bell rang, saving me from my friends' interrogation. For now, anyway.

As we walked towards the library doors, Ms P said, "Amy."

Her tone stopped me in my tracks. "See you guys later." My friends kept going, and I turned back to Ms P.

"We need to talk," she said, with a seriousness that made me wonder what kind of trouble I was in. "Which teacher do you have now?"

"Mr Feigel. Geometry."

"I need a word with you. I'll tell Feigel that you're helping me and you'll be late for class."

As she made the phone call, I racked my brain. Why would she hold me back from going to class? This wasn't like her.

When she got off the phone, she led me into her office behind the checkout desk and closed the glass door behind us.

"I know who he is."

"Wh-what do you mean?" I stuttered.

"I'll show you something. Please, don't take it personally.

72

We do it for safety reasons." She sat down and rolled her chair up to the desk. The Chicago Board of Education website was open on the screen. She closed it and clicked on an icon called SECURITY. It opened up a folder with several options: HALLWAY #1, HALLWAY #2, CENTRAL FOYER . . . all the way to STUDY ROOM #4.

No way. This couldn't be happening.

She clicked on STUDY ROOM #4 and the screen filled with a black-and-white image of the room. There was a faint buzzing sound, indicating that there was audio.

She pushed back from the computer and swivelled her chair to face me. "I'm sorry I invaded your privacy, Amy. But there was something different about that young man, and I wanted to hear the first bit of your conversation to make sure things were OK in there. I heard everything."

What could I say? She must think I was involved in some crazy role-playing fantasy.

"You're really convinced he's Alexander Banks, aren't you?" Ms P asked.

"I *know* he is."

"I'll admit that the moment I saw him, I thought of Alexander's picture on the book cover." She took off her glasses, folded them, and put them on the table beside her. "What proof did he give you that he's Alexander?"

I was momentarily fazed. Was she humouring me, or was she actually taking this seriously? "He has Alexander's scars, including the one on his tongue. It looks like someone tried to cut his tongue off, and it's not the type of thing you can fake. And there's something else. Friday night, when I got off the bus, I was attacked. Alexander saved my life. It was Vigo who attacked me."

Her hand flew to her mouth. She looked horrified — too horrified to be humouring me. I should glad that she believed me, but I wasn't. What I wanted was to hear her explain why none of this was real. Why Vigo couldn't possibly be here in Chicago killing innocent people.

"How do you know it was Vigo?"

"I caught a glimpse of his hair. And he made this strange growling sound. It had to be a vampire, because I got carried across the park in a second or two." It felt like the words were coming from somewhere else, a calm place outside of myself where I could talk about the attack without freaking out.

Ms P frowned. "And those two boys who were killed — that was Vigo." It was more a statement than a question.

"Yes. Alexander knows for a fact that Vigo is here. He chased him across the Michigan Avenue Bridge, and they ended up in our Chicago." I held my breath, still hoping that Ms P would say something to explain all of this away.

She was silent for a long time. "I told you that I did some graduate work, didn't I?"

I was startled by the change of topic. "You got a master's in physics."

"I might not have told you that I actually spent four years

working on a PhD, but was asked to leave the programme."

"No, you didn't mention that."

"I was asked to leave because my studies took me into an area of research that academia wasn't ready for. An area that *I* wasn't ready for, but one that compelled me, nonetheless: literary physics."

"*Literary* physics?"

"That's what I called it. I started out studying string theory, which is widely respected. String theory tells us that several dimensions coexist simultaneously. And I asked myself if it were possible for someone in our dimension to tap into what's going on in another one. Then I realized that it may, in fact, already be happening – in our literature."

I was trying hard to follow her. "Wait a second. You're saying that books are showing us what's going on in different dimensions? They're not really fiction?"

"Not *all* books. Very few, most likely. But haven't you read books that are labelled fiction, but have characters so real that you wondered if they might exist?"

"That's how *Otherworld* made me feel. That's how it made everyone feel."

"Exactly."

There was a noise outside, and we glanced towards the library doors. A harried teacher came in, corralling her students and barking at them to keep their voices down.

"Unfortunately, I have a library lesson this period," Ms P said, putting her glasses back on. "We'll continue this later. Can you and Alexander come over for dinner tonight?"

"I think so," I managed to reply.

Although I was dying to know more, I stood up. It would be better to continue the discussion with Alexander there, anyway.

Literary physics. It sounded crazy, but I knew Ms P, and she was anything but.

Seven

A few minutes before sunset, I knocked on the door to the den.

"Enter," he called.

I found Alexander sitting on the couch, already dressed and pulling on his socks. He tidied his hair with several well-placed rakes of his hand.

"You're up already?"

"I've trained my body to wake like clockwork at sunset."

"I hope you slept well."

He shrugged, not meeting my eyes. "Well enough."

I knew that Alexander was plagued by nightmares, and I'd bet he had just had one.

"On Sunday, I had a nightmare about vampires on my fire escape," I said, sitting down next to him. "In the dream, I actually let them in."

"The world of dreams is troubling that way." A haunted look flashed in his eyes. "You have no control."

He didn't elaborate, and I didn't push him.

"Ms Parker, the school librarian I introduced you to,

knows who you are," I told him. "She overheard us. Turns out there are cameras and audio in the study room. Creepy, I know. Like *1984*."

"What happened in nineteen eighty-four?"

I kept forgetting there was so much Alexander didn't know. "It's the title of a book I read in English class last year. It's about the government using technology to watch everything people do."

"You don't think you are in the book *1984*, do you, Amy?"

"No! You're the one from a book, not me."

"I was teasing you." A smile flashed across his handsome face.

"Oh." In the books, Alexander had only joked with his cousin James, and that was rare enough. "I guess I'm a little too on edge to get a joke. The whole situation scares me," I confessed.

"Good. Fear is a useful emotion for most people. It can save your life. Remember that."

"What about you? Is it a useful emotion for you?"

"Fear only saves your life if you're willing to run from your enemy." The haunted look returned to his eyes. "I ran from Vigo once, and I will never do so again."

"You were six years old."

"Yes. Logically I know that I was too young to do anything else."

Logically. But I bet that, deep down, Alexander still wondered if there was something he could have done to save his family.

His despair was palpable, and I was tempted to reach over and touch his hand, but I held back.

"You were saying, about the librarian knowing who I am," he prompted.

"Right. I told her what happened, and she believed me. It turns out she always thought something like this was possible."

"Indeed?"

"Yes. And she can help us make sense of it. We're going to her place for dinner. She's picking us up at seven." When I'd told Mom that Alexander and I were going to Ms P's for dinner, she was pleased. She must have thought that Ms P's good influence would lead Alexander to pursue college or something.

"All right, but I cannot stay long. My duty is to find Vigo before he kills again."

"Don't worry, we'll keep the visit short. You need to eat, anyway."

"Very well. I will defer to you on this occasion."

I had to smile. Alexander Banks deferring to me? Who'd have thought?

Fifteen minutes later, Ms P pulled up in her blue Honda Civic. I got into the front seat, and Alexander got into the back. "Nice to see you again, Alexander," Ms P said, turning onto the road.

"Likewise, Ms Parker."

"Amy tells me you've come to us from Otherworld Chicago."

She used the same conversational tone you'd expect from someone asking about your day.

"It seems so," he replied. "We don't call it Otherworld, but it is indeed the place depicted in the books."

"Do you find the books accurate, then, in their portrayal of your world and its people?"

"Mostly, yes."

"Mostly?" I turned back to look at him, not knowing what he was talking about.

"Elizabeth Howard's reports on events in my world are undoubtedly true. But she makes some character judgements that I do not agree with."

"Are you referring to the way she portrays you?" Ms P asked, glancing at him in the rear-view mirror.

"Yes." He shifted slightly in his seat, a clue that he was uncomfortable with the topic. "Although she does not say it outright, she clearly paints my character as misguided. A troubled soul bent on revenge. And, if you really want to know, I despise the way she portrays the courtship between my cousin James and that *thing*, Hannah. She describes it with such. . ."

"Understanding?" Ms P offered.

"Precisely! She obviously wants the reader to cheer for them. And she makes Hannah sound like – like a normal person."

"Just because she's a vampire doesn't mean she's evil, right?" I said. "There are some vampires who are working for peace."

Alexander scoffed. "The vast majority of them would sooner drink your blood than work for peace."

"Do you have any idea how Elizabeth Howard knows so much about your world, Alexander?" Ms P asked.

"No. Amy said you have some ideas on what is happening."

"I do." She drove into her driveway. "See? Here already. Let's get a bite to eat and talk more."

We followed her inside. Ms P's home was as charming and warm as she was. I'd been here a few times before, since she had Katie, Luisa, and me over for dinner whenever we stayed late to help with the library inventory.

After getting us glasses of lemonade, she put a roast chicken on the table, along with a bowl of mashed potatoes with carrots. "Dig in."

We passed the food around, loading up our plates. Once we were all a few bites in, Ms P said, "Tell me, do either of you know anything about quantum physics?"

We shook our heads.

"Quantum physics was my area of study back in graduate school." Ms P toyed with her potatoes to let the steam out. "It's the area of physics that studies the most fundamental level of existence – the quantum level. According to quantum theory, it is impossible to measure both the position and direction of any given particle."

The idea sounded familiar. "I heard something about that in physics class." Unfortunately, I didn't always pay attention.

"I believe that particles are, in fact, 'jumping worlds'; that is to say, subatomic particles are actually jumping back and forth between universes – or dimensions, if you'd prefer."

It was strange to hear Ms P talking this way. I knew she was really smart, but all this quantum physics was over my head.

"Wait a minute," Alexander said, holding up his hand to slow her down. "By dimensions, you mean two worlds unfolding simultaneously?"

"Yes." Ms P pushed up her glasses. "The number of dimensions out there is infinite. And because particles are jumping from one universe to another, many of these dimensions are remarkably similar to our own. But in your dimension, Alexander, there are vampires, and in ours there are not."

"The theory is plausible, but can you explain why Elizabeth Howard knows what is going on in my dimension?" Alexander asked. "Do you think she has found a way to travel between dimensions?"

Ms P shook her head. "I doubt that. I think some people are able to tap into parallel dimensions and write about them, often without knowing they are doing so. That is the essence of literary physics."

Alexander frowned. "You're saying that Elizabeth Howard *thinks* she's making my world up, but is really just seeing it?"

"Exactly. Other authors are potentially doing the same."

I tried to grasp this. So Elizabeth Howard didn't realize what she was doing? I couldn't wait until we could ask her in person.

"How is it possible that I crossed into this world?" Alexander asked.

Ms P took a sip of lemonade, looking thoughtful. "I would guess you were able to cross over in much the same way as subatomic particles. There must be a portal somewhere. The magnetic field of the portal kept your molecular structure intact. It's really quite amazing. Do you remember feeling an electrical surge when you were chasing Vigo across the bridge?"

"I don't think so, but I was full of adrenaline."

"If you retrace your steps, you might be able to find it again. I'll see if I can get my hands on a magnetic sensor for you. I still have some friends in the lab at U of C. The sensor should help you locate it, if it's still there."

"We're worried that Vigo might go after Elizabeth Howard," I told her. "She's revealed things about him that he wouldn't want anyone to know."

Ms P nodded gravely. "I hadn't thought of that. Even if he weren't angered by the books, there's a chance he'll try to track her down, thinking she knows a way back to Otherworld."

"She has a book signing in New York City on Saturday, and we're going to try to talk to her," I said.

"Good idea. I'll drive you. And if we're able to talk to her, I'll do what I can to lend some credibility to your story."

"Once she sees me, she will have all of the proof she needs," Alexander said.

But I wasn't so sure.

Eight

THE NEXT MORNING, I stopped into the library before my first class. Ms Finley, the art teacher, was standing in Ms P's spot.

"Is she OK?" I asked, alarmed.

Ms Finley smiled, obviously touched by my concern. "She's under the weather today. She said she'll probably be back tomorrow."

"Thanks." As I headed to my first class, I realized I should've expected that Ms P would take the day off. She must have been helping Alexander strategize. Last night, she'd offered her spare room and any resources she had to help him track down Vigo. I was relieved that he was going to stay with her. First of all, it would get Mom to stop asking so many questions about Alexander – I could tell her he'd found a place to stay. Plus, with all her knowledge, Ms P would be of more help to Alexander than I could ever be. Which isn't to say I wouldn't miss waking up and finding Alexander Banks in my home.

In bio, Katie asked, "Where'd you go last night? Did you get my message?"

I already had the lie prepared. "I went to Starbucks and some other coffee shops to give out some résumés. I didn't get your message until it was too late to call back." Guilt knotted inside me. I so wanted to tell Katie the truth, but last night Ms P, Alexander, and I had all agreed that Alexander's presence in this world had to be kept a secret. If word got out, the attention he would get could jeopardize his mission to stop Vigo.

It was too bad, though, because I knew I could trust Katie with anything. Luisa was a different story. She would never tell deliberately, but she had a way of letting things slip.

"I thought maybe you had a hot date with that Alexander guy," Katie said, grinning.

I wish. "We're just friends."

"Right *now*, you are," Katie teased. "I saw the way he looked at you. He totally has a crush on you."

I laughed — no, giggled. "You dreamed that up."

"I'm serious! I think he could be *the one*, Ames."

By *"the one"*, I knew that she meant my first boyfriend.

"Ha! You're blushing." Katie's hazel eyes sparkled.

"No, I'm not," I protested, feeling my face get hotter by the minute.

"Don't be embarrassed. It'll work out. He wouldn't have stopped by your school if he wasn't interested." She winked. "Hey, did you hear that Elizabeth Howard's going to be on *Evening Report* Thursday night?"

I shook my head, surprised. Elizabeth Howard rarely did interviews. "Are you sure?"

"Yep. They announced it on the *Today Show* this morning. Apparently she's been under pressure to speak out since the vampire murders."

"None of this is her fault. But I'm sure they'll give her a hard time."

"Exactly. It's stupid, if you ask me. No Otherworld fan would do something like that. Those books are deep and emotional." She hesitated. "Psychotic killers wouldn't be into that stuff, would they?"

"You never know. Maybe some guy wants to be like Vigo. We should be really careful."

Katie shuddered. "You're creeping me out."

If she only knew.

Since I didn't want to risk waking Alexander, I waited until sunset to call Ms P. By the time I called, he had already gone out on the hunt. Ms P told me she'd spent the morning teaching him to drive modern cars, since they both agreed that he could move around the city faster that way.

Ms P was back at school the next day, but had nothing new to report. Alexander was no closer to finding Vigo, despite using Vigo's equation of probabilities. We all knew what that could mean: Vigo had read the books, too.

And Elizabeth Howard was possibly in grave danger.

I kept feeling like I was waiting. Waiting for an update from Ms P. Waiting for news of more murders. Waiting for *something* to change.

I hadn't realized I'd been waiting to hear from Alexander himself until he called me before school on Thursday.

"Good morning," he said.

The sound of his voice made my heart race. "Hi. How are you?"

"I am well." There was silence for several seconds. "I was wondering if you would care to join me for dinner later this afternoon."

My pulse kicked up. It almost sounded like a date, although it was silly to think that Alexander would have the inclination to date these days.

"Sure."

"Is four thirty convenient for you?"

"Yeah, that's fine."

"Excellent. Until then." He hung up.

The day passed all too slowly. Everybody was talking about the *Evening Report* interview that night and what Elizabeth Howard might say. Would she deny that her books could have inspired someone to kill? Or would she look directly at the camera and appeal to the killer to turn himself in?

When I got home from school, Chrissy and Madison were watching a teen horror flick in the living room. I noticed the movie was nearing its end, which probably meant that they'd cut school for at least part of the afternoon. Mom had recently got a call from Chrissy's school about her ditching classes and had warned her not to do it again, but Chrissy didn't appear to be listening. Or maybe she *was* listening – to Madison instead of Mom.

"Hey," I said.

"Shhh!" Chrissy waved me away. It was a tense scene, with a willowy blonde exploring a basement with a flashlight. I definitely wasn't in the mood for horror movies right now. It felt like I was living in one.

Bypassing Chrissy and Madison, I went to my bedroom to start getting ready. Alexander would be picking me up in half an hour, and I wanted to look good. I kept the same faded jeans on but changed into a plum-coloured top. I also put on some eyeliner, mascara, and lipgloss, though I made sure to keep it subtle. The last thing I wanted was for Alexander to think that I was trying to impress him. But he *was* Alexander Banks, and I was, well, human.

I figured I'd wait for him in the lobby. At 4:25, I went back into the living room. The movie was over, and Chrissy and Madison were watching a talk show.

"I'm going out," I said, grabbing a jacket from the hall closet. "Tell Mom I won't be home for dinner. I should be back in a couple of hours."

"Do you have a book club meeting?" Madison asked.

She always referred to my friends as my "book club".

"No. I have a date."

It was worth it just to see Madison's eyes bug out.

Chrissy's head whipped around. "Is it that loser Alexander?"

"Maybe." And I walked out of the apartment, leaving her hanging.

OK, so maybe the date part wasn't true, I thought, as I pressed the elevator button. But I didn't regret saying it. What I did regret was that she'd probably tell Mom, and Mom would ask more questions about Alexander. Oh, well. It was still worth it to see the looks on their faces.

When I stepped out of the elevator, I saw Ms P's little blue Civic waiting out front. Alexander got out and opened the door for me, sweeping his hand gallantly.

"You look quite refreshed, Amy."

"Thanks." Had he just paid me a compliment?

The car stereo was pumping classical music. He turned it down when he slid into the driver's seat. "The cars of your world are remarkable. Such impressive technology. The seats and windows move electrically. And look, it even gives you directions." He pointed to the GPS.

"Are you sure you're OK to drive this?"

"Yes. The basic rules of driving are the same as in my world. Ms Parker was kind enough to give me some lessons. It has a manual transmission, which I am accustomed to. But if you would prefer to drive, you can."

"I don't have a licence," I admitted. We didn't have a car I could practise on, and it never seemed all that necessary. Katie and Luisa didn't have their licences, either.

Alexander drove carefully, and not a mile above the speed limit. "Ms Parker accorded me automobile privileges on the condition I avoid getting caught without a licence."

That made me nervous. "It's unlikely you'll get pulled over, but sometimes random people get stopped."

"If that happens, I can only hope that my new running shoes will help me evade the police."

I looked down and saw he was wearing the sneakers. I smiled.

We drifted into silence for a couple of minutes. I watched the city flit by the window, drenched in late afternoon sun. It was strange being in such a confined space with Alexander. Like the air was crackling with electricity. It was probably just me.

I cleared my throat. "Any leads on Vigo?"

"I have spoken to people who may have seen him in the downtown core. I would not be surprised if he struck there next. But that tells me nothing, of course, about where his hideout is located."

"At least he hasn't killed again."

I saw a muscle bunch in his jaw. "We can't be sure of that. He could easily have hidden his victims."

My heart sank.

"Maybe he went back," I said, vocalizing the thought as it came to me. "Maybe he knows about the portal and can travel back and forth. He could've led you here just to get you out of his way."

"That is a possibility. But my intuition says he's still here."

Intuition. In the books, it was given as much weight as science. And Alexander's intuition never seemed to lead him astray.

Within a few minutes, Alexander had parked at the kerb next to a Japanese restaurant called Genji. Did he even know what sushi was? The cuisine of Otherworld was traditional British fare, without many of the foods brought to the United States by twentieth century immigration. No one had dared to immigrate since the vampires came.

"Will this restaurant be satisfactory for you?" he asked, unbuckling his seat belt. "Ms Parker recommended it."

"Sure. I've always wanted to try Japanese food. You don't have it in Otherworld, do you?"

"No, but I thought I would try new things while I am here."

Strange. Alexander was a more adventurous eater than I was, and he'd only been in my world a short time.

I was about to get out of the car when he touched my arm. "Amy, I have one small request."

"Yes?"

"Please do not call my world 'Otherworld'. That is Elizabeth Howard's name for it, not mine. To me, it is simply Chicago. My home."

"I'm sorry."

He smiled. "Do not be sorry. Just understand."

We went inside. The restaurant's décor was minimalist, with small white tables separated by Japanese screens. Although our table was in the centre of the restaurant, the screens made it feel private. If I pushed my chair back a little, I could see the sushi chefs in the kitchen. Alexander positioned himself so that he could see the front door. I figured it was force of habit. Even though it was still daylight, he was on guard.

As if following my thoughts, he said, "I will have you home by sunset."

"About that, I was thinking—" I paused when a waitress came to fill our glasses with water. She asked if we would like something else to drink, and we both shook our heads. With his fork, Alexander removed the lime from his water and placed it on the table.

"I was thinking that I could help you," I finished. When he looked at me quizzically, I hurried on, "Another pair of eyes would be helpful, don't you think? I feel useless hiding at home while you're out there looking for him."

For a second, he looked like he was about to laugh, but then he saw that I was serious and he grew solemn as well. "You cannot help, Amy. Put that foolishness out of your head. You'd be nothing but a liability."

There it was: Alexander's trademark frankness. In the books, I'd found it refreshing; I could only imagine the freedom of being able to say exactly what I wanted. It wasn't so refreshing now that it was directed at me.

I wasn't going to go down without a fight. I took a long sip of water and faced Alexander again. "Earlier you said you've been questioning some people on the street about Vigo. I could help with that."

His expression darkened. "We are talking about a vampire, not some hooligan. I will not endanger your life just so you can feel useful."

If he'd put it more tactfully, I might have been touched that he cared.

"It is only a matter of time before Vigo finds out that I have been asking questions about him," Alexander went on. "What if he were to find out that a girl was with me? Who would be the easier target?"

"I see your point, but I wouldn't be wearing a name tag."

"True, but you must not underestimate Vigo. If he wanted to find you, he could. And I am not willing to take that risk."

I sighed. "I guess you're right."

"I *am* right. But I will say this, Amy. You're brave for a woman."

"For a woman?"

He cracked a smile, then started laughing.

I couldn't believe it. He was teasing me. Again.

Wasn't he too busy carrying the weight of the world on

his shoulders to joke around? Obviously not. I couldn't help laughing, too.

When our laughter subsided, we looked at each other, and there it was — a glimpse of the Alexander beneath. The one I'd always suspected was there. The one who was just an ordinary teenage guy.

Then he looked away, and his face closed again.

He ordered sushi rolls with fresh salmon, tuna, and eel, careful to avoid the spicy ones, along with pieces of shrimp, yellowtail, and sea urchin, with a side of sticky rice. I chose two vegetarian rolls, cucumber and avocado, and one California roll.

"I guess Ms P told you that Elizabeth Howard's going to be on *Evening Report* tonight," I said. "Are you going to watch it?"

"No. I will be out hunting by then. But I am intrigued to hear what she will say about the killings."

"Me, too."

When we got the food, Alexander veered the conversation away from anything vampire and on to my Chicago. He wanted to know how it had come to be so technologically advanced, how we chose elected officials, how much money we paid in taxes . . . and that was just the beginning. I was embarrassed that I couldn't supply more answers, but I tried my best.

"You've got a lot of questions," I said, polishing off my California roll — it turned out sushi was tasty. "Are you thinking of running for mayor of Oth— of Chicago one day?"

"Mayor? Good heavens, no. James possesses that ambition, not me. I merely have an incurable curiosity."

That curiosity was another aspect of Alexander that Elizabeth Howard hadn't discussed in the books. The more I spent time with him, the more sides of him I saw. And I felt so excited – privileged, even – to be getting to know him.

"Your world fascinates me, Amy. I couldn't have dreamed it up if I tried. So much innovation, so much opportunity. It is remarkable."

"It's nice that you see it that way. A lot of people think, with the economy as it is, there aren't a lot of opportunities."

"That's ridiculous. You are all extremely fortunate." He gestured with his chopsticks around the room, as if encompassing everyone. "Your people have never had to contend with vampires – at least, not until recently. You are not expected to marry so young. You are offered education. You have hospitals. A fairly competent police force, from what I have seen. What more could anyone want?"

His eyes were bright with passion, and a wave of sadness came over me. In my world, a guy his age would probably be going to college, partying, dating. Alexander didn't have those luxuries.

He'd spent most of his life conditioning himself physically and mentally to stalk vampires, and by the time he was sixteen, he'd garnered a reputation as the most fearless vampire hunter in Chicago.

One thing he did have was purpose. He had devoted his life to a noble cause – eliminating the vampires who posed a threat to his city. Part of me envied that he didn't have the confusion of wondering what to do with his life. But another part of me thought that confusion was an important part of growing up.

He was right that the people of my world were lucky. Suddenly all of my complaints about my city, my school, my life, my annoying sister, seemed trivial next to what the people of his world had to deal with.

No wonder Alexander thought that if one of our worlds was fantasy, it was mine.

As Alexander drove me home, the sun dipped behind the clouds, streaking the sky orange-pink. I wasn't ready to leave his company, but I knew he planned to have me inside before his night of hunting began.

Alexander stopped the car in front of my building. "Thank you for having dinner with me."

"You're welcome. I'll see you Saturday for the signing. If you need anything, call me. I'll have my cell phone on all the time, except when I'm in class."

"I have one, too," he said, pulling it out of his pocket proudly. "Ms P felt it was necessary."

I grinned at the sight of Alexander holding a cell. Who would have thought? "Great, then I can show you how to send a text message," I said.

"The sun will be setting in eighteen minutes. Six twenty-two, to be precise."

"It won't take long."

His phone was black and sleek, and much newer than mine. I clicked on his contact list. My cell phone number was programmed in, along with Ms P's cell, work, and home numbers.

"So, here is how you send me a text message. It's like a phone call but written down." I inched a little closer to Alexander, and when I felt the friction of his arm near mine, my heart pounded.

"Like email, then." Alexander nodded. "A message without paper."

"Right. You click on this until my number comes up, like you do when you're calling me. But instead of pressing Talk, you press this button over here." Looking up, I saw that his eyes were focused on my face, not the phone. I hoped I didn't have soy sauce caked on my cheek. I touched my face self-consciously. "Um, you with me?"

"Yes. Yes, of course." He gave his head a little shake. "You said a certain button."

"This button." I clicked it. "Now you type the message. It goes like this. Say you want to type *Hi Amy*." I typed it slowly, glancing up again to make sure he was following, and he was. "When you're done putting in the message, you press this button." I pressed it, and my phone buzzed in my pocket.

"Remarkable."

Taking out my cell, I quickly texted him back: **Hi Alexander**, and sent it. His phone beeped. He opened it and pressed a button to access the message.

"Now that I've messaged you back," I said, "you just need to press that button to reply. Go ahead."

He did, and very slowly typed in a few letters. Moments later the phone buzzed in my hand. I checked the message: **Goodd teaacher**

I laughed. "You're a quick learner."

He smiled. "You will have to teach me to correct my errors."

"It's OK. The point of texting is that it's fast."

"I see." His eyes drifted over my face, and I wondered if he was about to say something else. Then he seemed to snap to alertness. "Let me walk you inside."

I found my keys and got out of the car. He entered the lobby with me.

"I will contact you tomorrow. Goodnight, Amy." And he strode out the door before I could plead with him to be careful.

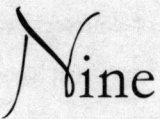

Nine

LATER THAT NIGHT, the *Evening Report* logo swirled across the screen.

"Good evening," the broadcaster, Rockland Philips, said in his deep baritone. "Tonight on *Evening Report*: one of the most popular authors of our time sits down with Teresa Curry. . ."

I settled back on the sofa as Elizabeth Howard's bio came on. I knew all of it already. She was forty-three years old and had "dabbled in writing" since she was a child. Studied Creative Writing at Illinois State and taught high school English. Married Patrick Howard, a businessman in the tech industry. Spent years juggling teaching, writing, and eventually, mothering two kids, before getting her first book published five years ago.

Not an unusual author bio. Nothing about psychic abilities or Otherworld channelling.

Next the camera settled on Elizabeth Howard, elegant in a stylish navy pantsuit, her brown hair perfectly arranged on her shoulders, her make-up flawless. She had the look of wealth and success and intelligence. But something about her eyes looked wary, even nervous.

The interview would be an hour long (with commercials, of course). I doubted they'd bring up the vampire killer controversy just yet – they'd hold their audience if they waited until later.

The first question had my ears perked right away.

Teresa Curry: "How did you come up with the idea for the Otherworld series?"

Elizabeth Howard: "I know this is a terrible answer, but I have no idea how I came up with it. I hadn't been planning on writing fantasy – the market seemed flooded with it already. But Otherworld and its characters just appeared in my head one day, and over the next few weeks, I couldn't seem to get rid of them." She pushed a lock of hair behind her ear, more a nervous thing than a necessity. "It didn't feel like I was creating Otherworld. It felt like I was looking in on what was happening there. I know some writers hate it when I say that, but it was all a very intuitive process."

Wow. Elizabeth Howard's explanation fit perfectly with Ms P's theory: the author was watching the events in Otherworld rather than making them up.

Teresa Curry: "Even though the series is meant for teens, your characters resonate with people of all ages. How did you manage that?"

Elizabeth Howard: "I'm not sure. James Banks appeared in

my head, this handsome young man who lived in a frightening world. I connected with him instantly. His heartache for Hannah, a beautiful vampire, was palpable. It was through James that I met all of the other characters, and eventually they started speaking to me directly, which is why I switched viewpoints. You could say the books developed organically. I would just sit down at my computer and watch events in Otherworld unfold."

Hmm. Interesting that she'd accessed Otherworld through James. That was natural, I suppose, since James was a kinder, more idealistic character who wore his emotions on his sleeve. Alexander, on the other hand, was reserved. You had to look twice as hard and listen twice as closely to know what he was thinking.

No wonder most readers gravitated to James.

The interview was interrupted by too many commercials. Footage of Elizabeth Howard at book signings was interspersed throughout, making me think she'd probably only sat down with Teresa Curry for all of twenty minutes. Finally, the interviewer edged closer to the topic everyone was waiting for: the vampire murders.

Teresa Curry: "Some are saying that your books have fostered a certain fascination with the occult and vampirism. How do you react to that?"

Elizabeth Howard: "My writing is pure fantasy, and should never be taken as more than that. Stories of any number of mythical creatures have been around since cavemen huddled in front of fires. My books are meant as entertainment, nothing more."

Teresa Curry: "What would you say to those who criticize you for glamorizing vampires and vampire culture?"

The author twitched. I could tell that got her back up.

Elizabeth Howard: "First of all, I don't think the vampires in these books *are* glamorized. Hannah wishes to be anything *but* a vampire, and refuses to drink human blood. As for Vigo, he's a sociopath. I don't think anyone would want to emulate him."

Teresa Curry: "But it appears someone is doing just that. Two teenage boys were killed in Chicago last weekend by someone, or more than one person, imitating a vampire. Your second book, *The Mists of Otherworld*, came out just one week prior. Do *you* think it's a coincidence?"

Elizabeth Howard: "I don't know. I honestly don't."

Teresa Curry: "If whoever committed these murders is watching now, what would you say to him?"

The camera zeroed in on Elizabeth Howard's face. It was a brilliant, heart-stopping moment. Suddenly she looked more like a deer in the headlights than a glamorous author.

Elizabeth Howard: "I'd tell him to turn himself in . . . so that he can get the psychological help he needs."

Vigo would not like hearing that. Not one bit.

The next day Katie and Luisa were buzzing about the *Evening Report* interview. My stomach kept flip-flopping as I thought of the New York book signing. I felt awful that I hadn't told my friends about it — they'd be so jealous if they knew I was going to meet Elizabeth Howard.

The plan was for Ms P and Alexander to pick me up Saturday morning at four thirty. If we didn't get slowed down too much by rush-hour traffic, we would be in Manhattan by the late afternoon. Since the book signing was at seven, we knew we wouldn't be able to get a legitimate place in line — we'd probably have to camp out for that — but we figured it would give Alexander enough time to find us a way in.

When I got home from school, Madison was over, as usual. She and Chrissy were painting their nails. I hadn't even kicked off my shoes when Madison asked, "Are you coming to the party tonight?"

I rolled my eyes. She wanted me to say "What party?" and then hear all about the party I hadn't been invited to. I wasn't going to play along. "Actually, no. I'm going to bed early because I'm heading to New York at four thirty in the morning."

Chrissy looked up from her nails. "Really? You didn't tell me that."

For a moment, I paused. Did Chrissy actually want to know what was going on in my life? "Elizabeth Howard's doing a book signing. Alexander and I are driving down." I chose not to mention that Ms P was coming.

"Hmm," Chrissy said. Which, from her, was approval.

Madison, however, didn't seem impressed. "We're going to

Brian Kowalski's. He's celebrating the track team's win. So, were you invited?"

Not this again. I didn't bother to answer. As I headed into the kitchen to grab a snack, Madison called after me, "Too bad! His parents are out of town and it's gonna rock!"

Then I heard her go "Ouch!" Chrissy must have elbowed her or something. Madison wasn't the sharpest knife in the drawer, so she hadn't clued into the fact that Chrissy wouldn't want me knowing that bit of information. She certainly wouldn't want *Mom* knowing it.

As I rummaged through the cupboards searching for a snack, I wished I could say something to stop Chrissy from going out tonight. Not only was a Brian Kowalski party bad news, there was a vampire out there. But I knew that if I tried to convince her to stay home, it would only make her want to go more.

I grabbed an apple and a handful of crackers, then headed to the computer. "I hope the party revs up before Chrissy's ten o'clock curfew," I said over my shoulder.

So this is what writer's block feels like.

Two hours later, I was still staring at the computer screen.

I thought that with Alexander Banks in my world, my fan fiction would flow like never before. Talk about wrong.

Now that I knew Otherworld was real, I couldn't go there any more. Whenever I opened one of the books for inspiration, all I saw was cold, dark reality.

Forget it. I'd try again another time.

I went to the kitchen, where Mom was making home-made mac and cheese. I knew it was her favourite comfort food because she tended to make it on Friday nights when she was staying in, and often accompanied it with a glass of wine.

"Smells good." I gave her a kiss. "Where'd they go?"

"She's having supper at Madison's." I could tell Mom wasn't too happy about that.

"More for us." Glancing at the darkening sky outside the kitchen window, I was glad that Chrissy and Madison had left well before sunset. But it would be dark when they headed to Brian's. I'd worry until Chrissy got home.

Mom must've been thinking along the same lines. "I gave her money for a cab. I don't like her taking the bus at night. Not with that crazy around."

Mom and I had dinner together at the kitchen table. It was just as well that Katie and Luisa were busy tonight – Katie had a hockey game and Luisa was rehearsing for a play next month – because I was too distracted to do much socializing. I listened as Mom told me about the latest drama at work. I reminded her that I was going to New York super-early tomorrow morning for the Elizabeth Howard signing, and Mom reminded me to call her when I arrived.

A few minutes before ten, Chrissy called.

"Honey, if you wanted to sleep over you should have told me before," Mom said into the phone, sounding annoyed. "You don't even have your pyjamas, do you?"

I signalled to Mom that I needed to talk to her. Now.

"Just a sec," Mom said to Chrissy, then turned to me.

I took a deep breath. "Madison told me they were going to a party. They might already be there."

I knew that Chrissy could hear me, but I figured there was no point in pretending. Had she really thought I would cover for her if she stayed out past curfew? I wondered about that myself. Maybe I would have, if I weren't so worried about her being out late with a vampire on the streets. Then again, maybe not. Thirteen is way too young for a Brian Kowalski party.

Mom's lips tightened. "Come home right away, Chrissy. And take a cab, as I told you."

I heard Chrissy whining into the receiver. "Don't argue with me, Chrissy," Mom said. "And you'd better be back by curfew or else you'll be grounded."

Chrissy's whining turned to shouting, and then a dial tone. Mom put the phone down, defeated.

"I can't trust a word she says any more," she said, shaking her head sadly. "She's changed so much since your father left."

I sat down beside her on the couch. "She needs more time to adjust."

"Your father should spend more time with her. With both of you."

She rarely talked about my dad, but I could tell she resented him. It wasn't fair that she had to handle Chrissy all by herself.

We sat there for a while, making little jokes about what antics

Chrissy might pull when she got home. Ten o'clock came around, and she didn't arrive. When eleven o'clock came, it was clear Chrissy had chosen to pull another antic entirely. The later it got, the more we worried. Mom called Chrissy's cell several times, but got no answer.

By midnight, we were downright panicked.

"Do you know where this Brian lives?" Mom asked me. "I'll get a cab there."

"Wait, I have an idea. Let me make a phone call."

From my bedroom, I called Alexander's cell.

He answered quickly. "Is everything all right?" I could hear traffic behind him.

"My sister's out way past her curfew, and Mom and I are worried. Where are you?"

"Fifteen minutes from your apartment. I'll be right there. Wait for me inside." He hung up.

I breathed a sigh of relief, then went back to the living room to tell my mom he was coming.

"He has access to a car? Great. Tell him I appreciate it."

If I picked up Chrissy from the party, it wouldn't be nearly as embarrassing as if Mom did. I hoped that would take some of the steam out of her anger.

When I got into the car a few minutes later, Alexander asked, "Do you know where she is?"

"I'm pretty sure she's at a party on Campbell Street. It's not far, just off LaSalle."

"I know where it is. Do we have any reason to believe she's in danger?"

"No. It's just that she got into a fight with Mom on the phone, and I wanted to make sure she got home OK. I hope I wasn't disturbing. . ."

"I didn't have Vigo in my sights," he said quietly.

As he drove, I had the strange realization that I'd missed him, even though I'd seen him just yesterday. Is that what love is, I wondered? When you want to be with someone every moment? The thought startled me. I'd fallen for the *character* of Alexander Banks, not the guy himself . . . right?

Within ten minutes, he'd turned on to Campbell Street.

"It's a big white two-storey. There it is. Two down on the left." I'd helped Katie deliver papers in this area a few years back. Brian's house was the biggest one on the block, and there'd always seemed to be a party going on.

The driveway was full of cars, so he parked a couple of houses down.

"I'll run in," I said. "It might take me a couple minutes to find her."

"I would like to come in as well."

I thought about it, and figured I could use the backup if Chrissy gave me a hard time. "Fine, but be nice, OK?"

"Of course."

We walked up to the front door and rang the doorbell. Nobody answered, probably because they couldn't hear it above the blaring music. I tried the handle, and the door opened.

The house was pretty dark and bursting with people. Red bulbs must have been put in the lamps, a pitiful excuse for atmosphere.

"Do you see her?" Alexander shouted in my ear.

I ducked my head into the living room, looking around. "I don't think so."

He let me lead. I squeezed through the people crowding the hallway. He took my hand and squeezed through after me. At the feel of his hand on mine, a giddy feeling swept through me. For a second, I let myself imagine what it would be like to be going to a party with Alexander as my boyfriend.

There were sweaty people everywhere, and I tried not to touch them as I moved forward. I glanced back to see Alexander, whose lips were pursed with disdain. Definitely not his sort of party.

I figured we'd check the basement, then the upstairs bedrooms. *If* we could even get through. There was a mass of people blocking the basement stairs, and no one paid any attention to my "Excuse me!"s.

Then Alexander stepped in front of me. With two big sweeps of his arms, he pushed everyone out of the way. Startled partiers stumbled back, falling over one another.

Some kid said, "Hey! What was that?"

Alexander glared at him. The kid cowered.

Taking my hand again, Alexander led me down the stairs.

The basement was even darker than upstairs, and it took my eyes a few seconds to adjust.

I walked up to one of the couches, scanning the people, catching sight of her long blonde hair. There she was, in a darkened corner. A guy was kissing her.

"Chrissy!"

She jumped. I recognized the guy from school. He was a senior named Reuben Torres, one of the jock squad, and a notorious girl-izer.

"She's in eighth grade, Reuben," I said, disgusted.

He shrugged. "So?"

I felt something hard shove past me. It was Alexander. He grabbed Chrissy's hand and yanked her to her feet. "Time to go home, Christina."

Reuben got to his feet. "Hey! What if she ain't ready to leave?"

Alexander looked him over. Then he placed a hand on Reuben's chest and nudged him. Reuben flew back into the couch.

Alexander waited to see if Reuben was going to come back at him, but Reuben was slumped on the couch, dazed.

I held on to Chrissy's arm and followed Alexander up the stairs and out the front door.

"Where's Madison?" I asked my sister. "We'll take her home, too."

"She wasn't feeling well, so she left," Chrissy replied, not meeting my gaze.

She slid into the back seat of the car. I noticed the skirt she was wearing – it was Madison's, and insanely short.

"Drop me off at Madison's," she told Alexander, like he was her driver.

"I'm dropping you off at *your* home." He power-locked the doors.

"What do you care what I do?"

"I don't concern myself with your tomfoolery. But your mother and sister do, and I am indebted to them."

She didn't miss a beat. "So are you actually dating my sister?"

I almost laughed. Chrissy knew she was in deep trouble, but she still had to get an update on my love life.

Before I could answer, Alexander said, "We have mutual admiration for each other, I hope."

I glanced at Alexander, my stomach somersaulting, then glanced ahead at the road.

"Mutual admiration?" Chrissy sneered. "What does that mean?"

"It means we have a lot in common," I said quickly.

"Oh, I get it. He's a big book nerd who doesn't have a life, too? Does he know you've never had a boyfriend?"

Thanks, Chrissy. He already thought I was odd for calling myself Mrs AlexanderBanks online. He didn't need to know that I'd never had a boyfriend.

"Your sister is brilliant and beautiful," Alexander snapped.

"Your childish behaviour is an insult to her."

Chrissy kicked his seat. "Whatever!"

Alexander didn't respond, only put the car in gear and drove off.

It was an awkward ride home, to say the least. The only sounds in the car were Chrissy's occasional grunts or seat punches.

Your sister is brilliant and beautiful. I wasn't naive enough to think he meant it. He'd obviously figured out that Chrissy saw me as anything but, and had wanted to come to my defence. Still, I couldn't deny the rush of pleasure I felt each time I remembered his words.

When we got home, Mom was standing in the living room, waiting. She took in Chrissy's skirt, and the relief on her face switched to anger. I knew she was going to let Chrissy have it, but first, she turned to Alexander.

"Thank you for picking up my daughter."

He gave a nod. "Think nothing of it, madam."

"He's psychotic!" Chrissy shouted, running to her room and slamming the door.

"I'll be right back," I told my mom. "I'm going to walk Alexander out."

"There's no need," he said, once we were on the other side of the door.

"I just wanted to thank you for helping me with Chrissy."

There was a strange look in his eyes, almost a question. And then he smiled. "At your service."

Ten

MY HEAD HAD BARELY hit the pillow when my alarm went off. Since I'd prepacked a bag of snacks for the trip, I just needed to dress, brush my teeth, get water bottles from the fridge, and wait in the lobby.

The car pulled up five minutes later with Ms P in the driver's seat and Alexander beside her. He got out to open the car door for me, and I caught my breath. He was wearing his clothes from Otherworld – the long coat, white shirt, trousers, and high leather boots. He was magnificent.

Instead of saying, "Wow," I managed to say, "Thanks," and get into the back seat.

"Morning, Amy," Ms P said, turning on to the road. "Alexander told me about your adventure last night. Guess you didn't get much sleep."

"I got enough." *Last night* was just four hours ago. Although I was tired, I was also pumped to get to the signing.

Alexander looked out of the window. "I was just commenting on all of the people about at this time of night. I am used to vampires owning the night. Only the vampire hunters dare to circulate before sunrise. Here, everyone seems so carefree. We just witnessed a group of adolescents singing in the streets, if you'll credit it."

"It's the weekend," I said. "I guess everyone wants to party."

"Have they no sense? They must know of the murders, yet they show no concern."

"Most people are desensitized to that stuff these days," I told him. "If it weren't for the vampire connection, the case wouldn't have got much attention. Just another murder in the city."

"That's astonishing," he remarked. "Perhaps it is due to the size of the population that such desensitization can occur."

"Here, we hardly know our next-door neighbours," Ms P said. "It's a shame."

"So tell me," Alexander said in a lighter tone, "did your mother give Christina a proper dressing-down?"

"She's been grounded for two weeks. I'm not sure Chrissy heard Mom say it, though, because she tried to drown her out with her music."

Alexander shook his head. "Such gall in one so young. To be 'grounded' means that she will stay in the apartment?"

"Yes. It means she'll have to stay home when she isn't at school."

"Why not deprive her of school as well?"

Ms P chuckled. "You can't just take a student out of school for two weeks, especially if they're under sixteen."

"Attending school is a privilege. It would be the perfect thing to take away from her."

"Chrissy doesn't see it as a privilege, trust me," I said. "She'd love to stay home for two weeks."

Alexander grunted. "In my world, that type of insolence is not tolerated. Then again, the consequences of staying out past curfew are very different. Someone who breaks curfew may never be seen again."

Hopefully it would never come to that here.

"At any rate, we can hope that your sister will mature. Thankfully, we won't have to worry about her being on the streets at night for a little while."

For some reason, I felt my eyes mist up. Alexander had said "we" wouldn't have to worry. He had no reason to care about my sister, especially after the way she'd treated him, but I was glad that he did.

From there, Ms P started asking Alexander questions about his world. He was happy to answer them, and launched into stories — ones that were not in the books. I gazed out of the window, watching dark fields flying by. Alexander had a rich, velvety voice, given to storytelling. I found myself conjuring up images of Otherworld, vivid images, and I wondered if this was what Elizabeth Howard saw. As I felt myself drift off, I heard Alexander whisper to Ms P, "I think she's sleeping. I'd better be quiet."

"Keep talking," I said sleepily.

I thought I heard him chuckle as he launched into a tale of a boyhood fishing outing with James. It was a cheerful story, and one that I knew wouldn't involve vampires.

"Good God," Alexander exclaimed, taking stock of the mass of people in front of the bookstore. We couldn't distinguish a line of any kind, just a huge crowd. This was very different from the scene outside the Book Nook when I'd got my copy of *The Mists*. This was chaos.

"We'll find a way," I said, my voice firm. I wondered if Alexander's determination was contagious.

Ms P dropped us off on the corner of Broadway and 82nd Street, then went to find parking. She was going to call my cell phone when she was back near the bookstore so that we could find each other.

We stood at the edge of the crowd, which had to number in the thousands. Alexander's gaze swept the area several times. Then he turned to me. "I'll have to leave you here. Ms P should be joining you soon. I must inspect this whole area to see what we are dealing with. I will be in touch by phone within the hour."

"OK. Good luck."

He hadn't moved five feet away when a girl spotted him and screamed. The group of girls she was with erupted in a chorus of screams.

"Oh my God, it's Alexander Banks!"

"Your costume is so perfect!"

"So gorgeous!"

"Can we get a picture? Please, please, please!"

Alexander turned to me, a rueful look on his face, and pushed past them into the crowd. I had to smile. If he didn't realize how crazed Otherworld fans could be, he'd realize it today.

Ms P called a few minutes later, and joined me on the street. She wore a square name tag identifying her as Lorraine Parker from the Chicago school district libraries. She thought it would lend her credibility when we got close to Elizabeth Howard.

As we stood there, the crowd kept getting bigger. No one nearby had a prayer of getting in. The only ones who did wore fluorescent green wristbands that actually had bar codes on them. I stopped a couple of people with wristbands to ask how they got them. One girl told me that her mom was a bookstore manager. Another pair, a teen and her mom, said they'd won them over the radio. Only two hundred people were going to get in, apparently. Even if we'd arrived last night and camped out, we wouldn't have had a chance. My confidence was starting to waver; with security so tight, how would we get in?

Soon after, Alexander called and told us to meet him five blocks down at a diner. When we got there, he was at a booth with a cup of tea, staring at a menu. He looked worn out. "Thank you for joining me here. I had to get as far away as possible from those hooligans."

His normally windswept hair was downright messy now, and there appeared to be a smudge of lipstick on his shirt. Ms P and I laughed.

"I *told* you your character was popular," I said.

"Yes, well, you were not exaggerating."

"Do you have a plan for how we'll speak to Elizabeth Howard?" Ms P asked him.

"I do," he replied absently, reaching into his pocket and placing three fluorescent wristbands on the table. "We just need to wear these and they will let us in."

Ms P and I exchanged a glance.

"I merely picked a pocket." He shrugged, like it was nothing. "I overheard a girl speaking on her phone, saying she was in possession of the wristbands."

"Poor girl, she'll be so disappointed," Ms P said, but she didn't hesitate to put on the wristband, and hand me one. "It's for the greater good, though."

"Do not have compassion for her. I don't." Alexander's mouth made a grim line. "She wore a shirt with Vigo's likeness on it, and on the back it said 'Vigo's Girl'. It's a complete outrage."

I was giddy. I didn't know if it was the excitement of being in New York City for the first time, or Alexander's presence. Probably both.

Because we had wristbands, we only had to go back an hour before the signing. The three of us spent the next couple of hours exploring. Alexander was awed by the skyscrapers, the traffic madness, and the streets crowded with harried New Yorkers and gawking tourists. He had been to Otherworld New York, but it was nowhere near as impressive as modern-day Manhattan. He wanted to stop and look at every billboard, every taxicab, every food cart.

As we made our way through the busy streets, Alexander took my hand several times. I knew he was trying not to lose me in the crowd, and that I shouldn't read more into it.

But I wanted to.

Eventually, we had to go back to the bookstore. With our wristbands, we were immediately let inside and pointed up the escalator to the second floor. It was a huge, multistorey Barnes & Noble, a real palace of books.

Even though we had come with a serious purpose, I could tell that Ms P was enjoying the atmosphere as much as I was. Alexander, however, took no amusement in all of the fans dressed up as James, Hannah, Vigo, and himself. As we jostled for a place in line, he muttered comments about how foolish they looked. It didn't help that several fans nagged him for pictures. He barked at them to leave him alone, but that only egged them on more, making them declare him the perfect Alexander Banks. Eventually, he gave up and scowled for a few pictures.

We happened to be standing near the Teen section. There was a display stacked with Otherworld books under a sign reading, TO LOVE OR KILL A VAMPIRE? And there was a picture of James and Alexander standing back to back. Hannah was in the foreground, blonde curls flowing around her, fangs bared.

Alexander rolled his eyes. "'To love or kill a vampire'? What the devil does that mean? There is only one way to deal with a vampire."

I shrugged. "It's supposed to be catchy."

"It's ridiculous, that's what it is. Who would love a vampire except my foolhardy cousin?"

"You can probably tell that a lot of people like Hannah," I said, gesturing to the crowd, many of whom were wearing curly blonde wigs.

"They would change their minds if they met her. Elizabeth Howard describes her as an angelically beautiful vampire, which is a contradiction in terms. Did she not notice her fangs? Or the skin that's as pale and thin as rice paper? But Howard never describes that, does she?"

It was true that most of the vampires I knew from books and movies were good-looking. It was all part of the fantasy. On the other hand, Elizabeth Howard wouldn't have called Hannah beautiful if she wasn't. And James must have seen something special in her. It was clear to all readers that Alexander had never given Hannah a chance.

A ripple of awe went through the crowd as Elizabeth Howard emerged from a back entrance with an entourage of six people, two of them security. Even from our vantage point, she gave the impression of elegance and poise.

Alexander stiffened when he saw her, a barely perceptible shift in his posture from straight to ramrod straight. For most people, she was a rock star author; for Alexander, she was the woman who had written about his life without his permission, and gained fame and fortune from it. I could tell that Alexander was smarting at the injustice.

The line moved steadily. A bookstore employee gave us copies of *The Mists of Otherworld*, and then a pretty, well-dressed young woman came up to us with a packet of Post-its, asking who we'd like the book addressed to. She had a name tag identifying her as Leslie Watson, from Elizabeth Howard's publisher.

Alexander frowned. "I plan on telling that to Ms Howard alone."

Ms P put a hand on his arm. "It's OK. They do it to speed things along, so that people don't have to spell out their names for her."

"If she can write such expansive prose, I imagine she can spell," he muttered, then turned to Leslie. "Very well. Have her address it to Alexander Banks. A-L-E. . ."

"I got that," she interrupted him with a flirtatious grin. "Great costume, by the way."

As we drew closer to the front of the line, I felt a rush of fan-girl excitement. Elizabeth Howard was only a few feet away. Under other circumstances, I'd be dying for her to sign my book, to pose for a photo with me that I could post on Facebook. But today wasn't the time for that.

Employees were ushering people past her quickly, which meant we'd have only seconds to make an impression. The plan was for Ms P to talk to her first, and give her a detailed note explaining our case. Then Alexander would introduce himself, and then me.

Suddenly Leslie walked up to us and pulled Alexander out of the line. "You next, *Alexander*. We'd like to take a few press photos with Ms Howard signing for you, if you don't mind."

I gave him a *don't blow this* look, and he inclined his head. "That would be lovely, thank you, Leslie."

Ms P and I held our breaths as Leslie ushered him up to the table.

"Hello, Elizabeth Howard," he said.

I wished I could have photographed her reaction. Her eyes widened, and she did a double take. Then she pulled herself together and managed a smile. "Hello."

A photographer approached and snapped some pictures.

"You recognize me, don't you?" I could hear the eagerness in his voice.

Elizabeth Howard smiled distractedly. "Alexander Banks, of course." She signed his book and slid it back to him, then looked over his shoulder, anticipating the next person, who happened to be Ms P.

"You don't understand," Alexander said, looming before her. "I *am* Alexander Banks, the real one. Do not say you don't recognize me, because I know you do. I can see it in your eyes."

Uh-oh. Alexander obviously felt he'd been snubbed by Elizabeth Howard, and that was *not* a good thing. I wished I could tell him to move along and let Ms P make our case, but he didn't appear to have any intention of budging.

Elizabeth Howard's eyes darted around, possibly for help. "Thanks very much, *Alexander Banks*," she said awkwardly. "You've done a nice job with the outfit. Who's next?"

"Wait," he said, holding his ground. "You, of all people, know me to never mince words. I came through a portal while I was chasing Vigo over the bridge. We must talk after the signing. All I ask is a few minutes of your time."

Elizabeth Howard gave him the kind of look that an orderly gives a mental patient who is about to crack. And then security descended on either side of Alexander. "Keep moving, son," said a burly security guard, taking his arm.

Alexander wrenched his arm away. "That is totally unnecessary, I assure you." He turned back to Elizabeth Howard. "You are in danger, Ms Howard. Vigo has crossed over, too."

The security guards grabbed Alexander's arms and yanked him away. With incredible strength, Alexander broke free and jumped in front of her. "Here is your proof!" He stuck out his tongue.

Her eyes bulged. Security grabbed him again, this time dragging him towards a side entrance. He didn't resist. In fact, he shot me a triumphant look.

Elizabeth Howard was pale and clearly shaken. A woman in her entourage had come up beside her and was talking with her quietly. Elizabeth kept shaking her head.

The crowd of people in the store — and the group of frenzied fans outside — were hooting and hollering, riled up by the scene Alexander had made. Ms P tried to inch closer to the table, but an employee stood in her way.

Elizabeth Howard got up and hurried towards the back of the store without even waiting for her entourage. Ms P climbed over a velvet rope and ran up to her, thrusting a note into her hand and saying something. Elizabeth seemed taken aback, but she accepted the note. By that time, her people were around her, and she soon disappeared out a back door.

About two minutes later, an announcement came on the PA, telling us that the signing had been cut short, and that Elizabeth Howard would reschedule soon. The crowd went ballistic, and it was all I could do to extract myself from the mass and claw my way out of the store.

I found a spot across the street and called Alexander's cell. He told me that he and Ms P were half a block away in front of a deli.

I darted down the street, meeting up with them a minute later. "Is it just me, or was that a total disaster?" I asked, out of breath.

"It might have appeared that way, but I know I struck a nerve," Alexander replied.

"You threw her off, all right," Ms P said. "Let's just hope it's because she believed you. I slipped her the note."

"I saw that." I managed a smile. "You were quick, Ms P. I can't believe how fast you jumped over the rope."

"I used to run track and field. Did I never tell you that?"

Alexander wasn't listening. He stared off at the downtown New York skyline, eyes fixed on some distant point. "Elizabeth Howard is in imminent danger. I know it."

No one in Otherworld questioned two things: Alexander Banks's determination, or his intuition. I hoped Elizabeth Howard would read Ms P's note and contact us . . . before it was too late.

Eleven

"WHAT WOULD YOU SAY is the probability that Elizabeth Howard will call us?" Alexander asked.

It was early the following morning, and the highway stretched before us. We'd been driving all night, but Alexander, of course, didn't need to rest. Ms P and I had taken turns sleeping in the back seat. Now, Alexander was driving and I sat beside him nursing an iced coffee while Ms P snored softly in the back seat.

I noticed that Alexander had used the term "probability". It wasn't a coincidence. To catch Vigo, he would have to think like him.

"You definitely had an impact on her," I replied, remembering the scene in the bookstore. "But you might have just scared her."

"I detect a note of disapproval in your voice, Amy. You believe I took the wrong approach, don't you?"

Usually I found it easier to keep quiet about things that bothered me, but I wanted to be straight with Alexander. "You should have taken a gentler approach. Ms P and I would have done the rest." I turned to him. "Has anyone ever told you that your behaviour can be a little extreme?"

"I've heard it a time or two." A grin pulled at the corner of his mouth. "But I'm not perturbed by your criticism, since you are already in love with me, Mrs Alexander Banks eight thousand and twenty-one."

I felt my temper flare. Of all the arrogant things to say!

"In love with you?" I exclaimed, trying to keep my voice down so as not to wake Ms P. "Give me a break! You're the most aggravating guy I've ever met. I'm not in love with you . . . and I never was." I spoke the words forcefully, as if that would make them true. But I knew it was far too late to guard my heart against Alexander Banks.

He was silent for several moments, watching the road. "I know. I was attempting to tease you. Perhaps it was a roundabout way of apologizing, if I did, in fact, go to an extreme. It's easy to call oneself in love with a character in a book because he is just a fantasy." His mouth curved without humour. "The real person is harder to accept."

I wanted to backpedal. Had I gone too far? I wasn't trying to say he was unlovable.

"You're not that bad," I said.

"I am inclined to believe you, except that even my dear cousin James calls me insufferable. He thinks I don't want to see him happy." He glanced at me. "What do you think?"

"He's wrong. It's obvious how loyal you are to him. I think James wonders if you want to see *yourself* happy."

He frowned. "Who says I'm not happy?"

"Hunting vampires can't be very fulfilling."

"Can't it? You don't know how satisfying it is to put a stake through the heart of a vampire who preys on innocent people. The truth is, killing vampires is the only thing that makes me feel anything close to joy. Grotesque, isn't it?"

It *was* grotesque, but it was also understandable. "After what happened to your family, maybe you can't feel happy unless you're preventing others from meeting the same fate."

"That is as reasonable an explanation as any I could have hoped for. Unfortunately, some would say that makes me misguided. A lost soul. Troubled. Tortured."

"Those are all words Elizabeth Howard used to describe you."

He grunted. "Indeed."

"You must want more out of your life than vampire hunting," I said gently. "Say you kill Vigo and return to your dimension, and James succeeds in having the vampires sign a peace treaty with the humans. Then what?"

"Would that it were so. But it sounds like a work of fiction."

"You must have interests other than vampire hunting. You said yourself that you have an incurable curiosity."

He paused. "The science of the body. I have always been fascinated by the play of tendon and muscle, the way the body adapts and strengthens due to a delicate balance of stress and rest. I think it would be a useful course of study."

"So that's why Helen said you should become a doctor. I always wondered where that came from."

"She had lofty hopes for me."

"You're only eighteen. Who knows what you'll be doing a few years from now?"

"Hunter to healer. Now *that* would make an interesting epilogue." But I could tell that he thought it was pure fantasy. "What about you, Amy? You, in this world of plenty, have countless options available. But I think you have already decided."

I stared at him. "Why would you say that?"

"I saw a stack of pages by the computer. I picked them up, thinking I was reading an excerpt of *Otherworld*, but then I saw your name attached to them. You're a writer, aren't you?"

Good thing he was looking at the road, because I felt myself blush. He'd *read* my stuff? I didn't talk about my writing aspirations a lot, not even to my friends. They knew I wrote fan fiction, but not that I had big dreams of being a published author one day.

"A lot of people write stories," I murmured. "It doesn't usually go anywhere."

"You will be different. Your work is vivid."

"That's because I write about your world."

"I disagree. It was the way you painted the scene that was

vivid. The words you chose. Your dialogue, especially, is razor-sharp. I think you should let the world see more of your writing."

Alexander's praise filled me with joy, but I pushed it aside. "Well, the world shouldn't hold its breath. I'm having writer's block."

"Perhaps it is a sign that you should write about something else – a world that is uniquely your own."

"I don't know if I'm ready for that."

He smiled as we exited the highway, nearing home at last. "I, for one, will be holding my breath."

When I got to school Monday morning, something was different. People stared at me, whispered when I walked by. I realized that this was about Alexander's performance at Brian Kowalski's party. Given our eventful trip to New York City, I'd forgotten about it.

But no one else would let me forget.

Luisa and I weren't at our lockers a full minute when two senior girls, Britney Palchek and Melissa Bennett, came up.

"So I hear your boyfriend beat up Reuben." Britney twisted her lips. "He should be careful because Reuben's really mad. So's Brian. When someone crashes his party and assaults his guests, he takes it personally."

"Reuben deserved what he got," I snapped back, startling myself. I was usually all about *avoiding* conflict. "He was going after my sister, who's in eighth grade."

"Oh, yeah? I heard she went after him." Britney smirked and walked away, Melissa in tow.

Luisa looked at me with a new respect. "Whoa, Ames. That was awesome. Tell me what happened Friday night! I can't believe you didn't say anything!"

"I didn't think it was a big deal." Which was true. Compared to everything else that was going on, the incident at the party was nothing.

I told her the story, and she cheered at the point where Alexander pushed Reuben.

"I'm so glad he put Reuben in his place. That guy is such a jerk. So, are you and Alexander official yet?"

"No. It's not that type of thing."

"Isn't it? Come on. He is a total hottie and you know it! Have you guys kissed?"

The thought of kissing Alexander sent a wave of heat through me. *I wish.*

"Well, have you?"

"No. We haven't."

"Darn. Don't let him get away. He's perfect for you."

I didn't say anything. We parted to go to our classes. I said hi to Ms Chau and walked up to my lab station. Katie was my lab partner. When she saw me, her face lit with excitement.

"I heard you and Alexander crashed Brian's party and he beat up Reuben!"

Wonderful. I had a feeling this was just the beginning.

As the morning wore on, I tried to ignore the talk swirling around me, but it was impossible. Kids who'd never spoken to me before demanded to know who my supposed boyfriend was and what school he went to and what exactly he'd done to Reuben.

But there were more pressing issues on my mind. We hadn't heard from Elizabeth Howard. If she'd believed Alexander, she probably would have contacted us right away, especially since he'd warned her that Vigo was in our world.

I wondered if the rumours I'd heard about her having writer's block were true, or if she was already working on the third book. If she was, maybe she could tell us what was going on in Otherworld right now, and if Vigo had managed to find a way back there. There was a possibility that Vigo had left this dimension, since no bodies had been discovered lately.

My mind turned over and over with questions, but I couldn't answer them without speaking to Elizabeth Howard. And I doubted we'd have another chance.

Lunchtime came, and I joined Luisa and Katie in the caf. Today's two-dollar feast was a hamburger and soggy fries. As I was about to start eating, I felt a sudden hush around me as Reuben and Brian approached our table.

My stomach sank.

Brian looked like a wrestler, muscular and compact, with a

buzz cut. "I don't like it when people crash my parties," he said, loud enough for everyone around to hear.

I didn't answer. I looked at my friends, warning them silently not to say anything.

Reuben, who tried to look cool with his spiky black hair and a soul patch beneath his lip, spoke next. "I shouldn't have bothered with your sister. She's such a cow."

I kept my eyes on my food, trying to resist the temptation to stand up and dump my ketchup-covered fries on his head. This would be over soon if I didn't give them any reaction.

"What's your boyfriend's name, huh?" Brian asked. "I want to know what makes him think he can come into my house uninvited. Unless you think he'd be too scared to talk to me."

I pictured a confrontation between Alexander and Brian. It wouldn't last long. I choked on a laugh.

"I should've messed him up when I had the chance," Reuben said.

Yeah, right. He'd been too dazed to get up after Alexander had pushed him.

"I hope your guy drops by the school soon," Brian added. "If he does, we'll be waiting for him. Tell him, OK?"

I could hear the anger in Brian's voice, and glanced over my shoulder, just to make sure he hadn't got any closer.

One thing was certain. Wherever Alexander Banks went, drama followed.

When I got home from school, Chrissy was alone for once. The upside of her being grounded was a blessed two weeks without Madison at our place. As soon as Chrissy saw me, she grabbed her bowl of popcorn and marched to her room, slamming the door.

I felt a knot in my stomach. Chrissy and I had spent most of our lives walking on eggshells during Mom and Dad's arguments. I thought the divorce would, at least, end the fighting and give us some peace, but it hadn't worked out that way. Chrissy persisted in getting angry about, well, *everything*.

She had left the TV on, and when I heard the introductory music of a special news bulletin, the knot in my stomach tightened. For a second I was even tempted to turn away.

"A young Irving Park couple was reported missing this morning. Though their names have yet to be released, it was revealed that they were last seen at a popular downtown club. . . "

An icy feeling gripped me. There was no doubt in my mind that Vigo had struck again.

"Hey," Alexander said as I got into the car. He smiled at his own use of slang, which made me smile back.

We hadn't seen each other since Sunday – only two days, but too long for me. I was glad he'd texted me this morning to ask if I'd have an early dinner with him. Although I knew he got along well with Ms P, I figured he liked having a friend his own age. Maybe it put a bit of normalcy into his crazy life.

"I saw a small restaurant around the corner." He manoeuvred the car into traffic.

Uh-oh: he meant Mac's Diner. People from school hung out there, and that was the last thing we needed.

"I know a better place," I said. "It's just a few blocks further. I should warn you not to drop by my school again unless it's an emergency. A couple of the jocks from the party are looking for you."

His eyes lit with mischief. "I'm flattered."

"Well, I like to stay out of trouble as much as possible." I gave him a serious look. "It's better if you stay away."

"Are you concerned for my safety?" There was a twinkle in his eye.

"No. In an ideal world, I'd love to see a smackdown between you and those guys. But I know you don't want more attention, and everybody at school is already wondering who you are after what happened Friday night."

"I take your point. Let me know if you change your mind."

The Burger Barn was quiet at this time of day. We chose a booth and slid on to the cushioned seats. As the waitress approached to take our order, I saw the flush in her cheeks when she looked at Alexander. Even in his casual clothes, he was striking to look at. It wasn't just that he was uncommonly handsome; his presence altered the atmosphere of any room he entered.

When the waitress left, Alexander grew solemn. "You heard about the couple," he said.

I nodded. The latest news report was that the bodies had been found — with the distinctive neck wounds.

"Are you sure it's Vigo who did it?" I asked. "Not some other vampire who might have crossed over?" I hated vocalizing the thought.

"There is no one but him. I am quite certain of that. His methods are distinctive. He usually takes two victims at once, and he prefers young blood. Most vampires are more random. Most vampires, I would have caught already."

"Do you think he'll start changing people here into vampires?" It was another horrible thought, but I had to ask. The process of changing a human into a vampire — by having a human drink the vampire's blood — was described in detail in *Otherworld*.

"Vampires believe they are bestowing a great gift when they change someone into their kind. It is to give them eternal life, after all. I do not think Vigo will change anyone unless he has some greater plan to populate your world with vampires."

Seeing my horrified expression, he put up a calming hand. "I doubt Vigo is ready to share this mortal playground with anyone just yet."

I hoped he was right.

We got chilli burgers and potato wedges. Since I'd only had a couple of bites of my lunch, I was ravenous. Alexander watched with amusement as I made a mess. I didn't see how he managed to eat his burger without globs of chilli falling out. I had to ask for extra napkins.

By the time we'd finished, it was five o'clock. Since we had more than an hour until sunset, I suggested we drive to a park on the riverfront.

When we got there, we walked past a play structure and headed for the rocky riverbank. Alexander tested some of the large rocks to make sure they were stable, then he walked out a bit from shore.

To my surprise, he turned back and extended his hand to me.

I took it, carefully walking out to stand on a rock next to him. He was staring at the horizon, seemingly lost in thought. The sun was an orange circle of fire above snowy white clouds.

"This would be a beautiful place to watch the sun set," he said. "In my world, it's hard to appreciate a sunset. Violence so often comes with the darkness. And the vampires feed off our misery." His eyes skimmed over the rippling water, then the unruly shrubs, plastic bags, and bits of garbage lining the shore. "I know this riverbank. I used to spend time here when I was a boy." There was a ghost of a smile on his lips. "It's a pleasant spot."

As I stood on the rocks with him, it felt like we were living one perfect moment. I didn't know how much time I would have with Alexander Banks, but I knew this moment would stay with me for ever.

"What are you thinking?" he asked.

"I'll tell you some other time," I said, knowing it wasn't true. Knowing I would never have the courage to tell him how I felt about him. Knowing that it would just add another burden to his shoulders.

He accepted my answer. But his eyes held mine, wistfully, as if he had a thousand secret thoughts of his own.

Then we stared at the horizon for a long while.

"I found the portal." He spoke towards the sky.

I snapped out of my reverie. "You did?" Why hadn't he said something sooner?

"I believe so. I retraced the route of the chase several times with a magnetic sensor Ms P procured for me. There is a certain spot near the base of the bridge that consistently scored off-the-chart readings. There was also the slightest shimmer that told me I was in the right place. I didn't get close to it, however. I don't want to go through accidentally, in case it were to close and prevent me from coming back."

I felt a pang in my gut. If Alexander accidentally crossed back to his world, unable to return. . . I didn't want to think about how I'd handle it. "Could that happen anytime? I mean, could the portal just close?"

"Yes. Ms P has likened the portal to an overlap of our

dimensions. There is no telling how long it will remain open, or if it might shift position. We will be monitoring it closely."

"Are you worried that the portal will close and you'll never be able to go home?"

"I have wondered about it. I am more worried that I won't stop Vigo."

Usually Alexander was all bravado, but now he was being real. I was seeing the true Alexander Banks, the one Elizabeth Howard had only hinted at.

His eyes were intense, misty from the wind. "I know I can catch him. I know it in the core of my soul. But what if it isn't meant to be?"

I turned away from him, wishing he'd never said the words. It was the same fear I'd had from the beginning.

"I'm not afraid of death, Amy. I think there's peace beyond. If there's such darkness here, it stands to reason that there must be light there. Aunt Helen always talked about the spirit world like it was as real as the physical world. She thought my family would be there waiting for me." He turned to me. "But if I die without killing Vigo, what purpose would my life have had?"

I didn't know how to answer that. I just said, "You are *not* going to die."

But I didn't know if it was true. I only knew that if he died, a part of me would, too.

Twelve

I HAD COMPLETELY FORGOTTEN about Luisa's birthday.

Which made me feel like an awful best friend.

On Saturday night, she was having her Sweet Sixteen. We'd be going to the new teen-only dance club that had opened a few months ago. It was called Club Teen Scene, an embarrassing name, but we'd heard it was awesome, and Luisa was totally excited about it.

Before Luisa's cousins and drama club friends were due to arrive, Katie and I went to her house and spent a couple of hours hanging out and getting ready. They made me laugh a lot, Luisa with her theatrical flourishes and Katie with her deadpan humour. I was surprised that I could laugh so much despite the weight on my mind. Maybe I was laughing because of it. After all the stress of the last few weeks, I needed an outlet.

After the other girls showed up, we ordered Chinese food, then had birthday cake. It felt wonderful to be normal again, and I tried not to let the idea of going out at night frighten me.

Luisa's parents drove both of their cars to drop us off at the club. When we got in, I was impressed. The club was huge, with multicoloured lights overhead. Luisa was in her element, immediately rushing out on to the dance floor and throwing her arms in the air. Katie and I followed, laughing. This was much better than our school dance had been. A huge screen at the front of the club showed the videos that went along with the music. Sometimes the DJ – or VJ, I guess – turned a camera on the crowd, and we could see ourselves dancing on the screen. Luisa loved it, and did her craziest moves whenever the camera swung our way.

After dancing for a while, Katie, myself, and two of Luisa's cousins sat down at the tables in the back. I was having more fun than I'd thought possible, and Luisa, well, she was still going wild on the dance floor. The only thing missing was Alexander. I wished he had the luxury of taking a night off, of being a teenager for a change.

Too wired to keep sitting, I went to buy a soda.

"Hey."

I turned to see a red-haired guy with a shy smile.

"You go to Ridgefield, right?" he asked.

"No." The quickest way to let him know I wasn't interested was to avoid direct eye contact. So, trying to look bored, I glanced over his shoulder towards the tables.

And I froze.

There was a guy sitting there – young and pale, silvery-blond hair.

"Something wrong?" the guy beside me asked.

I didn't reply. I couldn't.

It was him.

Vigo Skaar was sitting at one of the tables with a can of Red Bull. His eyes drifted over the room.

I ducked my head, moving behind the guy who was talking to me. If Vigo saw me, he'd see my fear, and he'd know I recognized him.

It surprised me that Vigo's face didn't look cunning, or evil. It was boyish. An innocent face.

The guy next to me was talking again. I pulled out my cell phone and dialled, still positioning myself between his shoulders.

Alexander's phone rang. Once. Twice. *Please, please, answer the phone!*

Three times. Four.

The voice mail picked up. *The customer who has subscribed cannot—*

I hung up. Dialled again.

Alexander's line rang again. And rang. And rang.

With shaky fingers, I texted him: **vigo here. club teen scene. 101 adams st.**

The police. I had to call the police. And then I had to get my friends out of here.

I hurried to the bathroom and called 911.

"I'm at Club Teen Scene." I hardly recognized my voice. I sounded hysterical. "The vampire killer is here!"

"Miss, calm down, has anyone been hurt?"

"No, not yet. Please hurry!"

"How do you know he's the vampire killer, miss?"

"I—" I didn't know how to answer that. "He has these fangs. I know it's him. Please send the police now!"

"Don't worry. They'll be there soon."

She believed me. My panic said it all.

"Where is the suspect now, miss? Can you describe him for me?"

"Silver-blond hair, black jacket, looks about eighteen. He's at the tables at the back. Hurry, please! I have to go. My friends are in there."

I hung up. Alexander still hadn't called back. Where was he? By the time he saw my text, it would be too late.

I forced myself to walk, not run, out of the bathroom. I felt my heartbeat thumping louder than the bass. Vigo hadn't moved. He was sitting in the midst of about twenty potential victims, all drinking their sodas and chatting away with no idea who was watching them. Katie was among them, and so were Luisa's cousins.

I went up to their table, grabbing Katie's hand. "There's a fight going on outside – it's crazy stuff, you guys have to see it!"

They needed no more encouragement, and headed for the door. I went with them, but stopped to grab the sleeve of a security guard in the doorway.

"Don't look now," I muttered, "but there's a guy at the back tables who I think is the vampire killer. He's the blond one drinking Red Bull. He's wearing fangs."

The security guy, skinny and not much older than twenty-one, scowled. "If this is a joke—"

"It's not. Are there more security people around?"

"Yes." As he reached for his radio, I stepped in front of him so that Vigo wouldn't see. "He could look over and see you. Call from outside."

It took no convincing. He went outside and got on his radio.

"Ames! I don't see—" I heard Katie calling, but I ignored her. I had to get Luisa out of there, so I headed towards the dance floor, watching Vigo out of the corner of my eye.

I saw him move. He was slowly getting up from the table, his eyes focused on a trio of girls. I knew he was going to strike.

He lunged, his black jacket spreading out like wings behind him. I screamed.

From another direction, someone else lunged, slamming into Vigo, sending him sprawling across the table.

It took me a second to realize that it was Alexander.

A wall of people ran towards the fight, and I had to jump out of the way to avoid getting knocked down.

Alexander slammed Vigo's head into the table. Vigo kicked and writhed like a wildcat, not giving Alexander the chance to free one hand to grab the stake.

Two cops rushed in, guns drawn. Vigo stilled under Alexander and turned his head to the side, sobbing like a child.

Alexander used the moment to pull out his stake. He raised it.

"Drop it or we'll shoot!"

The cops weren't going to shoot Vigo, I realized. They were going to shoot Alexander.

I jumped in front of them. "No!"

I heard a shout, and then something hard slammed into me. And I was out.

$\mathcal{T}$hirteen

IN THE STILLNESS OF my bedroom, something had changed. I wasn't alone. The grey mist of dawn lightened the window shades. My eyes swam into focus. Alexander was there, sitting on the edge of my bed. His shirt was blood-spattered, his hair messed up.

Last night came rushing back to me: Vigo. The police. Alexander knocking me out of the way. How I'd blacked out for a minute after falling to the ground, and then opened my eyes to see Alexander being restrained by the police . . . and Vigo gone. Luisa and Katie had helped me up and rushed me out, frantic. Luisa called her parents so they could pick us up and take me straight home. I'd been in a daze, barely able to make sense of anything.

"I'm sorry to have wakened you," Alexander whispered. "I just wanted to make sure you were all right."

"I'm fine," I said, sitting up. I'd never been so happy to see someone. "Did you break out of jail?"

"There was no need. Once you left, I broke free of the police and went after Vigo. But he was long gone."

"I can't figure out how you got there so fast."

Alexander set his jaw. "I had already tracked Vigo to the club. He had lined up with everyone else, bold as brass. I had to find an alternate entrance. I ended up having to enter through a third-storey window."

"I don't understand it. Why would he attack with so many people around?"

"He wanted to make a scene. A horrific scene." Even in the shadows of my bedroom, I didn't miss the hard glint in his eyes. "You almost got yourself killed, Amy."

"*Me?* What about you?"

"I was poised to kill Vigo."

"And the police were about to shoot you. If I hadn't jumped in—"

"If you hadn't jumped in, Vigo would be dead. I had to let him go in order to prevent you from being shot."

"You think you could have staked him before they shot you?"

"Yes."

"But as soon as you drove the stake into him, they would've opened fire on you!"

"Very likely."

I stared at him, unable to believe what I was hearing. "And that would've been OK?"

"Vigo would be dead, and that is all that matters. I would have fulfilled my destiny."

"It's not your destiny to die!" I said it with such force that my head throbbed.

"How can you know that?"

"I just do. That's why I stepped in."

"Vigo knows about you now," Alexander said quietly.

I pictured Vigo, and felt a stab of fear. His skin was smooth and pale, so pale that he'd reminded me of a sick little boy, someone you'd want to comfort, not run from. I'd seen him play the helpless card when Alexander had been about to stake him. How many people who had helped Vigo had paid with their lives?

"He doesn't necessarily know that I *know* you, right?" I asked, hearing the tremor in my voice. "I . . . I could've just been some person not wanting to see anyone get shot."

"You jumped in front of police with their weapons drawn. He knows, Amy."

I glanced towards the window. "He can't come in, right?" I remembered my dream about letting the vampires in, and shivered.

"Unless he is invited, he can't come in. Let your mother and Chrissy know that they are not to let a stranger into the apartment under any circumstances."

I nodded, and Alexander watched me for a moment. I suddenly felt self-conscious in my thin T-shirt and pyjama bottoms, my hair wild around my shoulders.

"You put your life on the line last night," Alexander said softly. He searched my face. "Why, Amy? Why would you do such a thing?"

Tears filled my eyes. "You know why."

"No, I don't know."

I swallowed hard. *"Your love is your greatest vulnerability,"* Alexander had said to James in *Otherworld*. The truth of his words struck me then. I loved Alexander – not the character any more, but the real person. I'd known it ever since that evening on the rocky riverbank. And I was more afraid than ever that something bad would happen to him.

I spoke before I could stop myself.

"I love you, OK?"

He looked stunned. "You love me."

I dropped my eyes. My heart was beating erratically. "Yes."

"You don't have to look away, Amy."

I raised my eyes, dashing away tears with my knuckles. "I don't have any more to say about it, so please forget it."

"I will. But just one thing."

He leaned into me, and his lips closed over mine. For a moment I was too shocked to respond. Alexander Banks was kissing me. Was this a dream?

My lips parted, and I kissed him back. His hand slid into my hair, bringing me closer.

This definitely wasn't a dream. His kiss was nothing like the tender, romantic kisses of my fantasies. It was better. I could feel the roughness of his stubble against my cheek. I tasted a ravenous hunger inside him that matched my own.

When he finally pulled back, I saw a burning look in his eyes.

We didn't speak for a while as we both tried to regain the control we'd lost.

"Forgive me," Alexander said.

I wanted him to kiss me again, but I wasn't sure I could speak. Or move.

He reached out, as if to touch my face, then dropped his hand. "I must go." He stood up, and left the room.

When I awoke again, it was almost noon, and someone was knocking on my door.

Mom peeked in. "How are you feeling?"

For a second, all I could think about was Alexander's kiss. And I realized, with a sense of wonder, that I felt happy — happier than I'd ever been.

But that wasn't the answer Mom expected. I'd come in last night, pale and shaky, and told her I wasn't feeling well as an excuse for not sleeping at Luisa's.

"Much better," I said, yawning. "I think I was just overtired."

"What happened last night?" Mom asked, looking concerned. "A few of your friends called this morning asking how you were doing. Luisa said there was an incident at the club and you got caught in the middle."

"It's not a big deal. Just a stupid fight. I got knocked down." I saw Chrissy hovering in the doorway, curious, if not concerned.

When she realized that I had spotted her, she straightened and walked away.

"Let me bring you breakfast in bed," Mom said. "Pancakes? Waffles with bananas?"

"I'm not hungry yet. But thanks, Mom."

She kissed the top of my head.

I got up to go to the bathroom, then came back and checked my messages. They were all from the girls, pelting question after question.

I called Luisa.

"Ames! Oh my God, how are you?"

"I'm OK."

"What happened? None of us understand. Katie said that you told her a fight had started outside. Next thing I know Alexander's beating up some guy in the middle of the club and then he's getting arrested!"

"He didn't get arrested. The cops went after the wrong person. Some guy randomly started hitting people. Alexander helped the cops take him down."

"Are you sure? Amy, be honest with me. Has Alexander been stalking you or something? Is that why he showed up last night?"

"No. It was nothing like that. I told him he could meet up with us at the club. Anyway, I'm so sorry your Sweet Sixteen got ruined."

"My birthday didn't get ruined. For once I was actually there when something exciting happened. I'm just sorry you got banged up."

"I'm fine. Don't worry about me."

When we hung up, I sat back against my pillow. I wished I could stop lying to my friends. One lie always seemed to need more lies to back it up. And the troubling part was, I was becoming better at it, quicker. It wasn't exactly a skill I'd been hoping to develop.

But if I was becoming a better liar, how could I have let the truth slip to Alexander? I still couldn't believe I'd told him I loved him. I hadn't meant to. It wasn't like me to speak without thinking. But the words had just slipped out. Why?

It was a good question. But the question that really drove me crazy was: why had he kissed me?

Luisa must have relayed the message that I was OK and needed my rest, because no one called again. Tomorrow I'd face more questions at school, but I wasn't going to worry about it. I had plenty of other things to worry about.

Midafternoon, I was flipping through a magazine on the living room sofa, still obsessing over the kiss, when there was a knock at the front door.

"I'll get it!" Chrissy said, running out of her room.

"No, wait!" Panicked, I jumped off the sofa, beating her to the door. "We didn't buzz anyone in."

"So? It's easy to get in the building." She looked through the peephole. "Oh." She went back to her room.

I looked through, then opened the door. "Hey, Katie."

She didn't come in. I could tell something was wrong. She never looked this serious.

"We've got to talk." She glanced behind me, spotting my mom in the kitchen. "Maybe we should go somewhere and get coffee?"

"Sure." I got my wallet and a hoodie. A quick check of the clock told me it was almost three – plenty of time before sunset.

The elevator was crowded, but we squeezed in. Two old ladies with hearing aids were talking loudly about how kids these days were all messed up and into weird cultish stuff and no wonder there was a vampire murderer out there.

Outside, the afternoon sky was overcast. Gusts of wind stirred the sidewalk litter. There weren't many kids out. They were probably snuggled on couches watching Disney movies.

Katie thrust her hands into the pockets of her jeans. "Should we head to Starbucks?"

"I don't need anything. You?"

"Nah. Let's not bother, then."

We went to a nearby school yard, grabbed a free bench. A group of guys were playing basketball, and I couldn't help but think of the poor teens who'd been murdered while playing ball last week.

Katie turned to me. "I need the truth."

"The truth about what?"

"Last night. Everything. First, you're rushing us out of the club with some excuse about a fight outside. There *was* no fight outside. Next thing I know, there's a brawl going on between Alexander and Vigo."

I blinked. "What?"

"I was watching through the window. Those guys looked exactly like them. Alexander had a stake, and he was about to kill Vigo when you jumped in front of the cops. Did I imagine all that?"

My stomach tightened and I looked down. I wasn't sure what to say.

"You need to tell me the truth. Or tell me I'm insane. Just tell me *something*."

I wasn't going to tell her she was insane, not after all she'd witnessed. And she was one of my best friends. It was time I told her the truth.

And so I did. I told her everything, the words coming out in a flood. I started with the night I'd been attacked by Vigo, and explained how Alexander had convinced me he was real. I told her all about Ms P's theory, and even the trip to New York City to meet Elizabeth Howard. I only left out the part about Alexander kissing me in my room, and my profession of love.

When I was done, Katie had a dazed look in her eyes. "This is crazy, Ames. Crazy. Like science fiction."

"Or literary physics."

She half-smiled. "We always knew Ms P was a little eccentric."

"So you believe me?"

"I do. If I hadn't seen what I saw last night, I might not. But. . ." She shook her head. "You were wicked brave, throwing yourself in front of the police."

"I don't feel wicked brave." *I feel wicked scared.*

"He doesn't know who you are, right? Vigo, I mean."

"No." I heard my voice waver. "I don't think so."

"Good." But I saw a flash of worry in her eyes.

"Katie, I'm so sorry I didn't tell you what was happening. I really wanted to. But we didn't want Alexander's presence here to get out. It would interfere with him hunting Vigo."

"I don't blame you for not telling me." She exhaled deeply, and I guessed what she was thinking – that she might have *preferred* not to know.

"Please don't tell Luisa," I added. "She's not great at keeping secrets."

"I know. It's going to be hard, but I won't tell her. I promise."

I gave Katie a hug. Tears came to my eyes as I realized how lucky I was to have her as a friend. I wished I'd been able to confide in her sooner.

"So," Katie said after we separated. "I can't believe you met Elizabeth Howard. She freaked out when she saw Alexander, huh?"

"Sort of. She seemed to recognize him at first, but then she didn't believe his story. It was Alexander who freaked out when she wouldn't listen to him. You know how temperamental he is."

"I do. That's why I prefer James." Suddenly Katie's face lit up. "Hey! If Vigo and Alexander are here, do you think James might cross over?"

I had to smile. "I wish he would, especially if he brought Hannah with him. We could use a vampire on our side right now."

At school on Monday, Reuben and Brian came up to me. "Heard your boyfriend got into another fight this weekend," Reuben said, leaning against my locker. "They say he jumped some kid at the Teen Scene."

Jumped some kid? If they only knew.

"I bet he's too scared to fight guys his own size." Brian crossed his arms to show off his pecs. "Next time he won't have a choice." Brian bumped fists with Reuben, and they walked off.

I sighed. I'd barely been at school five minutes, but the story had already circulated. I didn't know if I had Luisa or her drama club friends to thank, or someone else from our school who'd been at the club.

"Teach them a lesson, Ames." Katie poked her head around the door of my locker. "Not everyone's got *you know who* in their corner."

"Don't tempt me. If Alexander gets involved, it'll only make things worse."

"I think they'd be so scared of him they'd never bug you

again." Katie grinned. "It would be sweet to see Alexander kick some butt. We could call it AlexanderBanksMania and sell it on pay-per-view."

I couldn't help but laugh.

The morning droned along. My thoughts kept returning to the weekend. The terror at the club. My realization that I loved Alexander, and speaking the words out loud. The kiss — and what an incredible kiss it was. But then I would think of Vigo still out there, and any happiness I felt was replaced by fear.

At lunch I headed to the library. Ms P jumped off her stool when she saw me.

"Are you all right?" she cried. "Alexander told me what happened Saturday night."

"I'm fine." I followed her into the inner office, where we could talk privately.

"He told me that the police had their guns drawn and you got in the way." Her voice was stern. "What were you thinking?"

"I had no choice — they were going to shoot him."

"I know how fond you are of Alexander. But you could have been killed."

"I didn't think the police would shoot me." The truth was, I *hadn't* thought. I had acted on instinct.

"Events are unfolding as they're meant to, Amy. You shouldn't have interfered."

I stared at her. "Do you think Alexander is meant to die?"

A troubled look came over her face, and she put a hand on my shoulder. "We have no way of knowing how this will end. If Alexander has to give his life to kill Vigo, it might be for the greater good." Behind her glasses, I saw tears come to her eyes. "I would hate to see anything happen to Alexander, but he's chosen this life for himself. And sometimes . . . sometimes those we love best end up dying."

I shook my head. I could not accept what Ms P was saying. Alexander was *not* meant to die, and I was *not* going to regret saving him. "The story isn't going to end that way. I know it, Ms P."

"The truth is, Alexander doesn't belong in our world. You know that, don't you?"

"No. I don't know it." I wanted to cry, but I couldn't. The sadness was locked inside me.

"I'm sorry I've upset you, dear. I only want you to be safe."

"I'll be fine."

"You always say that, even when you're not fine," she said gently, and I knew that some part of that was true. "Vigo has seen you now, so you must be extra careful."

"Don't worry. I won't be going out after dark."

"Good. Keeping yourself safe has to be your number one concern."

"I know. Trust me, Ms P. I don't have a death wish."

That night, as I was getting into bed, Alexander phoned. It was the first I'd heard from him since our kiss, and my heartbeat sped up.

"Elizabeth Howard just called me in hysterics," he said.

I gasped. "Is she OK? Is she hurt?"

"She is traumatized, but not injured. Vigo came to her door this evening with a huge arrangement of flowers. He asked her son if he could come in. But when Elizabeth saw him, she recognized who it was immediately."

"Oh, God." I pressed a hand to my forehead, feeling dizzy. Poor Elizabeth.

"She addressed Vigo by name, then he bared his fangs and lunged at her. But he was unable to enter her home because he hadn't been invited. He fled."

I could only imagine the terror of it. No wonder Elizabeth Howard had been hysterical.

"What did you say to her?"

"I told her that she and her children were safe in the house. Her husband is away in California on business. I promised that I would visit her tomorrow, and that we would find a way to keep them safe. She lives in Kenilworth, just an hour from here. At any rate, I will call Ms P when we hang up. I am sure she will want to come with me tomorrow. She can probably leave right after the school day ends."

"Me, too. I'm coming, too."

$\mathcal{F}$ourteen

"THAT'S IT, seventy-one Oak Drive," Ms P said the next afternoon, pointing to a white house at the end of a cul-de-sac. It looked like all the other houses on the block, except its lawn was shaded by an unusual amount of shrubbery and trees. I wondered if it was the result of rabid Otherworld fans trying to peek in Elizabeth Howard's windows.

The neighbourhood surprised me. It was affluent, with large new-looking houses, but it wasn't ultra-posh. With her millions, I'd have pictured her living in a hilltop mansion.

We got out of the car and walked up to the house. Alexander pressed the doorbell. After a few moments a voice came through the intercom. "Yes, who is it?"

"Alexander Banks and my friends Amy Hawthorne and Ms Parker."

"I'll be right there."

Seconds later the door opened, and Elizabeth Howard greeted us with a fragile smile, ushering us in. In jeans, a mint wool sweater, and not a speck of make-up, she looked different from the glamorous author she'd been at the book signing. But she still gave off an air of elegance and intelligence. She showed us to the living room. "Please, come in."

A girl with brown pigtails ran up and skidded to a halt in front of us. "Hi!"

We said hi back. The girl giggled and ran away as quickly as she'd come. I could hear the beeps and explosions of a video game coming from another room.

"I kept them home today," Elizabeth said. "I know it's daylight but . . . I just couldn't."

Her living room had taupe walls and cream couches, stylish but homey. The mantel was filled with pictures of her children and some older people, probably her parents or in-laws.

Although the room had huge bay windows, the shrubs blocked out a lot of light, making the atmosphere sombre, even though it was a sunny day. We sat on the couch and she sat on a loveseat across from us.

"Thank you for coming." Elizabeth's hands were tightly pursed in her lap, maybe to stop them from trembling. I could see the smudges of fatigue under her eyes.

In many ways, I felt like I already knew Elizabeth Howard. But she didn't know me. Judging from the way she was looking at Alexander, though, she felt a familiarity with him. He was one of her characters, after all.

"I'm sorry I didn't believe you, Alexander," she went on. "On some level I think I did, but it was too hard to grasp."

"You shouldn't apologize," he said gently. "*I* would like to apologize for being so forceful."

She managed a smile. "I wouldn't have expected anything else." She looked from Alexander to me, then to Ms P. "How did this happen?"

Ms P took over, diving into an explanation of literary physics. Watching Elizabeth's shocked face, I worried that the information was too much for her to take in at once. She listened, spellbound, as Ms P completed her explanation.

"So . . . you're saying that I didn't make up Otherworld at all," Elizabeth Howard said slowly. "That I somehow tapped into another dimension?"

We all nodded.

Her eyes clouded, as if she was remembering. "I knew that something special was happening. I've been writing since I was a child, but the writing process of the Otherworld books was like nothing I'd known. Normally I would spend hours dabbling with different scenarios, plots, characters. But when I got the idea for Otherworld, it took off immediately. It was like the story was already there, and I just had to write it down." Her face paled. "This must mean . . . I'm a fraud. To think that I won the Los Angeles Times Book Award last year. If I'm not really creating Otherworld, maybe I should give it back."

"You're not a fraud," I said firmly. "You wrote about the events of Otherworld perfectly."

"*Did* I?" She looked at Alexander.

He nodded. "You've done us justice, Elizabeth. But you are a little too psychic for your own good." I knew it took a lot for him to say that, especially since he considered her books a complete invasion of privacy.

"Have you had psychic experiences before?" Ms P asked.

Elizabeth considered that. "I've always been intuitive, much to the annoyance of my husband. Take me to a party, and if there's tension between two guests, I'll know it, even if they're across the room from each other. Ever since I was a kid, I've picked up on thoughts, feelings."

"You're an empath," Alexander said. "It's a well-known skill in my world, as you know. My aunt was the same way."

"Helen," Elizabeth said softly. "I was thinking of her the other day. You know, I always thought it was strange. I didn't want her to die, but no matter how I tried to write it, her death was inevitable."

I saw a muscle twitch in Alexander's jaw. "She was a fine woman, my aunt."

"She loved you so much, Alexander. She saw you as a son."

He didn't meet her eyes. He changed the topic. "I'm quite sure I've discovered the location of the portal. It is at the base of the Michigan Avenue Bridge. Our only problem now is Vigo."

The mention of his name sent a tremor through Elizabeth. "You know what he and his coven have done to your city, Alexander. It's just a matter of time before he does it to ours."

"I have every intention of finding him and killing him, once and for all," he said, a hard edge to his voice. "But in the meantime, you are not safe."

"I know." She had a pleading look in her eyes. "How do I keep my family safe?"

To my surprise, Alexander got up and walked over to sit beside her, taking her hand. "You're going to get through this," he assured her. "But you must leave town immediately."

"My sister-in-law has a cottage on Lake Superior. Maybe we can go there."

"That's not good enough. You have to go somewhere where you have no connections, a place he can't possibly anticipate. Your choice should be random, somewhere you've never been to before. And your husband will have to join you there. Or else he can be used as bait to reel you in. You know Vigo."

"Far better than I want to." The frightened look in her eyes said it all. "My husband will never believe what's happening, though. I think I told you, he's in LA on business. I called him in a panic last night, but he thinks I'm just having an anxiety attack over the third book. Whenever I try to start it, all I can see are James and Hannah searching the streets for some trace of you, Alexander." She paused for a few seconds. "I've got threatening emails in the past. Maybe I'll tell my husband that the threats have escalated and that the police suggested we leave town for a while."

"Good," Alexander said. "You should go overseas. It's unlikely that Vigo will pursue you there. Here, you were easy targets, being so close to Chicago. But he's enjoying terrorizing Chicago too much to leave now. You're not worth that much to him."

"I hope you're right. I just don't understand. . . Why does Vigo want to kill me?"

"You have exposed his insecurities, not to mention the probabilities method he used to evade me. And there may be another reason. Killing you would create a media sensation and give him the notoriety he craves."

"I— I see." I saw her pretty features start to crack.

"We'll take you and your children to the airport," Alexander said. "Within a few hours, you'll be safely out of the country. Now you'd better go pack."

"Right." As she was leaving the room, she turned and looked back. "Be careful, Alexander. You're the one he really wants. Your death would be . . . the ultimate prize."

"Yes, I know." If he was afraid, his face gave nothing away. "He and I will be meeting soon."

In the couple of days since our visit to Elizabeth Howard, no more murders were reported. But I felt little relief. I doubted that Vigo would go much longer without killing.

Stay inside after dark. I had to remind myself of that when I was going stir-crazy. It wasn't that I didn't often stay home on weeknights. It was the fact that I *had to* stay inside that made me feel caged. I found myself tempted to walk the one block to the deli, but then an image of Vigo would enter my mind, and the temptation vanished.

Vigo wasn't just a villain in a story any more. He was a menace who could be lurking around any corner – in a park, at a club, or on your doorstep . . . as Elizabeth Howard had discovered.

When I asked if Alexander could spare some time late Thursday afternoon, he agreed to pick me up at four. It would be our first time alone together since we kissed. I felt nervous but excited to be near him again.

As I climbed into the car, my heart leaped at the sight of him. His hair was damp, and his skin had the glow of someone who'd just showered. He looked strong, healthy. Like someone powerful enough to stake vampires.

I noticed a gym bag in the back seat. "Did you work out?" I asked.

"Yes. I slept this morning so that I could train this afternoon. What would you like to do?"

"We could go to the park."

He agreed, and drove to the one we'd been to before. The autumn afternoon was cool, but clear and blue-skied. We found a bench near some swings.

"How do you train to hunt vampires?" I asked.

"For the most part, I practise fighting with the most skilled people I can find. Lately I have been training with a few fighters at a gym downtown. They call themselves mixed martial artists."

"Oh, yeah? How did you talk your way into training with them?"

"I simply offered to show them my skills."

I grinned. "Are you serious?" It occurred to me that Katie would love this. Maybe she was right about having AlexanderBanksMania on pay-per-view.

"Why wouldn't I be serious? I must do whatever I can to find the best partners possible."

"Did you kick their butts?"

He frowned. "The buttocks are among the least sensitive places to hit someone."

I laughed. "It's a figure of speech."

"To kick butts. Interesting." Alexander seemed to make a mental note of this. "What we do, mainly, is grapple," he continued. "The idea is to get your opponent on the ground in the quickest time possible. Vampires are too strong to be bested by a human's physical strength, you see. One needs speed, skill, and enough endurance to last thirty seconds."

Wow. He really had this down to a science. "Why thirty seconds?"

"A fight with a vampire rarely lasts longer than that. Most

last under fifteen. Ideally, I'll have the vampire on the ground with a stake through his heart before he even knows what hit him. If it doesn't happen that way, I must take control within thirty seconds. After thirty seconds of intense fighting, any human will start to tire. That's when the vampire's superior strength and endurance give him the advantage. Then you'd better run."

"Has that ever happened to you? Have you fought longer than thirty seconds?"

"Yes, when I was younger. I insisted on starting to hunt before I was ready. No one could talk me out of it." He rolled up his sleeve, revealing two pea-sized scars on his forearm. *Fang marks.* "This is the result. I was fighting a female vampire who had been terrorizing my neighbourhood. Because she was small, I thought she'd be a straightforward kill. Of course I was wrong. The fight lasted much longer than thirty seconds, but I refused to give up and run. I thought that in just a few more seconds I could stake her. I was weakening, but I had so much adrenaline that I didn't even realize it until her fangs had sunken into my arm."

"How did you get away?"

"I didn't. Another vampire hunter staked her in the back."

"Good thing he was there."

"Yes, well, the vampire hunters I had trained with knew that I was in over my head. I was just thirteen. I cherish this scar, though. It reminds me not to be stupid." He rolled his sleeve down again.

"That's a good story. I'm surprised it's not in the book."

"I should have thanked Elizabeth Howard for that. Perhaps she was trying to protect my pride."

"That, or the story about your tongue being slashed by a vampire's blade was better."

I was enjoying our banter, and I could see that he was, too.

His dark eyes fixated on the cement beneath our feet, and I could tell he was thinking about something else. "You're enchanting, Amy," he said after a moment. "I am privileged to have met you."

I felt my face getting hot. *I* was enchanting? He had it backwards. I glanced at him, suddenly wondering if he was thinking about the kiss.

He took a breath. "I don't know how well you remember what happened on Sunday morning."

I stared down at the bench, at the inches of space between us, my heart thumping in my ears. "I remember."

"I tried to avoid it coming to that, but it was bound to happen." I looked up, and his eyes flickered to mine, as if he was uncertain as to whether to keep going. "My attraction to you has tested my self-control and my concentration."

My mouth felt desert-dry, but I nodded. Alexander Banks was attracted to *me*.

"What are your thoughts?" he asked, looking at me intently.

My mind went blank. "I don't have any."

He gave a startled laugh, and it broke some of the tension. "I'm not sure that we should act on this, Amy. It is up to you. If you tell me to keep my distance, I will. But if you don't, I warn you: I might kiss you again."

"Might?" I was being bolder than I'd ever been. But if he was thinking of kissing me, then I wanted him to. Needed him to.

He swallowed. "It's probable."

"It's . . . fine with me."

"Are you sure?"

"Yes, I'm sure."

Instantly, he leaned in to kiss me. Our teeth knocked together. "I'm sorry," he muttered.

"It's OK."

He smiled against my mouth. Then he proceeded to kiss me with such heart-stopping thoroughness that I felt like I'd been transported to heaven.

Eventually he pulled away. "Forgive me . . . I had thought to attempt a chaste kiss." He searched my eyes. "I did not mean to put your reputation at risk."

Still dazed from the kiss, it took me a few moments to understand what he meant. Kissing and courtship were taken a lot more seriously in his world. If you kissed a girl in public – or if you were caught spending time with her in private, kissing or not – you'd better be ready to marry her.

"My reputation will be fine," I said with a smile. "It's your reputation you should be worried about. You're *the* Alexander Banks, after all."

"I'm terribly concerned." A grin tugged at his mouth. "I was a winning catch on the marriage market, but you have destroyed me. I'm afraid the only way to salvage my reputation is to bring you back with me and make you my wife."

"If I have to." I was kidding, too. *Mostly* kidding. For a second, I wondered what it would be like to go to Other-world with Alexander, to be the girl he would love and protect for ever.

His face suddenly went serious. "In truth, in my world, I would never be able to associate with someone of your charac-ter. Vampire hunting has left my reputation beyond repair. It is considered manual labour of the most appalling kind. People want it done, but they don't want to know those of us who do it."

I shook my head at the idea of Alexander being undesirable. "Well, in my world, someone of my character would be lucky to date someone like you."

His dark gaze glittered. He picked up my hand, lifted my wrist, and kissed it reverently.

I closed my eyes, feeling the warmth of his lips against my skin. I'd read about James doing the same thing to Hannah. In their world, kissing someone's wrist was a sign of repressed passion.

When I opened my eyes, he lifted his lips from my wrist and curved them into a smile.

$\mathcal{F}$ifteen

ON FRIDAY AFTERNOON, I sat in front of the computer, unable to write a word.

This was ridiculous. I needed to write. It was my sanity, my way of releasing all of my pent-up emotions. Instead, I felt like I was in a creative deep freeze.

As usual, Alexander was all over my mind. His kisses had imprinted themselves on my soul – I relived them again and again. He was *the one*, I realized. The one I would always love. The one that no other guy could ever measure up to.

Katie and Luisa arrived around six, which forced me to get up from the computer. I had invited them to sleep over, hoping some time with my friends would distract me from everything that was going on.

I made our favourite dinner: grilled cheese, bacon, and tomato sandwiches. Luisa brought the movie *Fool's Gold*, since she worshipped Matthew McConaughey second only to James Banks.

Mom joined us for the movie. I invited Chrissy to join us, too, but her only answer was to shut her bedroom door in my face.

The movie's story line was so ridiculous that we decided it was funny. Mom, on the other hand, gave up halfway through, opting to watch TV in her room. We noshed on chips, and once we'd satisfied our salt fix, switched to brownies for our sugar fix.

After the movie, we chatted about random topics – whether Jake Levine was worthy of Luisa, and whether Katie and I would pass our upcoming biology test. Luisa wanted to talk about all things Otherworld, but I managed to steer the conversation away with Katie's help. We turned on MTV. There was going to be an interview with Noise Pollution, a band Chrissy loved. I knew she'd be disappointed if she missed it. Since I didn't feel like being ignored, I asked Luisa to tell her. "She won't want to watch it with us, but Mom will put it on for her."

Luisa got up. "You're too nice." And she headed down the hall.

I really wasn't. But if I did a few nice things for Chrissy, she might stop giving me such a hard time. She was too good at holding a grudge. After two weeks, she was still giving me the silent treatment, still slamming doors, still clanging dishes.

Luisa came back. "Chrissy's not there."

"She must be in with Mom. Hang on." I went to Mom's room and opened the door to find Mom dozing in front of the TV. No Chrissy.

Puzzled, I looked towards the bathroom, but the door was open. I turned to my friends, my alarm growing.

"She must've gone through your room and climbed down the fire escape," Katie said, wide-eyed. She knew about Vigo, knew the threat that lurked outside when the sun went down.

I rushed to my room and found my window open. "Unbelievable." Chrissy's grounding ended tomorrow, and she had to go and risk messing it up now? What was she thinking?

I grabbed my phone and called Chrissy's cell, but the voice mail picked up. No surprise there. I texted her: **Come home now or call. I haven't told Mom.**

Luisa read the text over my shoulder. "You're not going to tell your mom?"

"We'll see. I know how to get Chrissy home." There was no need to panic yet. Madison's cell number was written on the white board in our kitchen. I dialled it.

"Hello?" Madison answered.

"It's Amy."

"Oh." It sounded more like an *uh-oh*.

"Chrissy snuck out. Is she with you?"

"No. I'm home sick on a Friday night and it sucks. It's not exactly where Chrissy or anyone else would want to be."

I could hear the congestion in her voice, but that didn't mean Chrissy wasn't there. "My mom doesn't know she's gone. If you have Chrissy call me within five minutes, I won't tell her. If she doesn't call, Chrissy will be grounded for at least two months this time."

"Seriously, she's not here," Madison insisted. "I'm not lying."

"Then where is she?"

"I don't know."

"Forget it. I'm telling my mom."

"No – wait! She was going to the AMC cinema."

"Who was she going with?"

There was a pause during which Madison was probably thinking up a lie.

I gritted my teeth. "You'd better tell me, Madison. If you don't, Chrissy's going to blame *you* for getting her in trouble."

"OK, well. . . She's meeting some guy she met on the Internet."

I could hardly believe what I was hearing. Was Chrissy insane?

Seeing the astonished look on my face, Katie and Luisa exchanged worried glances.

"What's his name?" I demanded.

"Justin."

"Tell me everything you know about him or I swear—"

"I don't know much, all right? He's seventeen, I think, and he goes to the Catholic school. She met him on Facebook."

"Did she show you his profile?"

"Yeah."

"Find it and send me the link. *Now.*"

"Fine. But you'd better not tell your mom, or Chrissy will kill me. I can't believe you're making me do this."

I hurried to the computer. I wanted to see if this guy's profile looked legit. I was terrified that this seventeen-year-old was really twenty-five with tattoos and a criminal record.

"OK, I sent it," Madison said. "Can I go now?"

"Wait. I want to make sure it went through."

I checked my email every few seconds until I got it. I clicked on the link, and the profile came up.

It was a blond guy holding up a glass of red liquid. Ice blue eyes stared straight into the camera lens.

The air escaped from my lungs.

A strange numbness set in, without panic or emotion. My mind kicked into high gear.

I grabbed my wallet and took off at a run. Katie and Luisa were shouting after me, but I wasn't listening. I didn't wait for the elevator. I ran down the stairs, flew. One hand coasted the railings while the other held up my phone, clicked on Alexander's number.

He answered. "Amy—" But the connection was lost. My phone never got reception in the stairwells.

Seconds later, I burst out the doors of my building and called him again.

"Amy?"

"Vigo's got Chrissy."

"What?"

"He lured her on the Internet. She was meeting him at the AMC cinema. It's the huge one downtown on Michigan Avenue."

"I'll meet you there." He hung up.

I ran several blocks to LaSalle Boulevard and couldn't see any cabs. I kept running, glancing back every few seconds. Finally I saw one, and I ran into the middle of the street, jumping up and down like a crazy person.

The cab screeched to a halt. I got in. "AMC downtown. Hurry, it's an emergency."

The cabbie looked startled, but he pressed on the gas.

The night flew by the window, not fast enough. Never fast enough. I didn't know who would get there first, me or Alexander. I didn't know where he was when I called. If I found Chrissy with Vigo, what would I do – attack him?

And if I didn't find them there?

Those were the longest minutes of my life. When the cab finally pulled up to the kerb, I threw a twenty into the front seat and ran through the doors of the theater. Alexander was there, interrogating the girl at the ticket kiosk. He stepped back, saw me.

"We have to check the theaters!" I shouted.

"There is no need." His face sobered. And I saw something I'd never seen in his eyes before. Fear. For Chrissy, I realized. "They're not here. The ticket girl said they met in the lobby but left together immediately."

"Are you sure?"

"Yes. I showed her the picture of Vigo from the book cover. She identified him right away."

"Where did he take her?" I looked around helplessly, wanting someone to point me in some direction, any direction that would take me to Chrissy. "Where do we go?"

"I don't know."

The look in his eyes told me everything.

Chrissy could be dead already.

The world blurred. I tried to stay in the land of numb, to keep the hysteria bottled up.

But when we got into the car, I doubled over and sobbed. I should have known that Vigo would attack where I was most vulnerable. I should have warned Chrissy, protected her.

Alexander held me for a minute until I calmed down. Then he dropped me off at home and took off to look for Chrissy.

The police came, and I showed them Vigo's Facebook profile. When the officers saw his picture, they exchanged a look. It was obvious to me that his picture matched the description of the vampire killer that had already been circulating. Thankfully, the connection didn't seem to register with Mom. She was already on the verge of falling apart; she didn't need to know the whole truth just yet.

Morning came. Mom encouraged Luisa and Katie to go home and get some sleep. They agreed. But Katie came back with coffee and bagels a few minutes later. She wasn't leaving my side.

Mom went to the police station to fill out reports and give them more pictures of Chrissy. I kept waiting for the phone to ring. It would be Alexander telling me he'd found Chrissy and she was fine. Or Chrissy saying it was all a misunderstanding and she was on her way home. Or maybe the door would open, and there she'd be. She could have got away from Vigo.

Morning bled into afternoon. The land line rang. I jumped at it. Katie ran up beside me.

"Hello?" I said, my heart beating in my throat.

"May I speak with Amy?" asked a smooth male voice.

"That's me."

"A formal introduction is long overdue. My name is Vigo Skaar."

I caught my breath. Katie immediately wrapped an arm around me, as if sensing who it was. I couldn't even process that I was speaking to the vampire himself.

"Wh-where's Chrissy?" I demanded.

"Here with me, of course. She's sweet, your Chrissy. I can smell the sugar in her blood. Would you like to speak to her?"

"Yes."

There was a pause and then, "Amy, help me!" It was definitely Chrissy.

"You're going to be fine, Chrissy. Just—"

"I am glad you have faith that she will be fine," Vigo said.

"Please let her go."

"As much as I'd hate to give up this sweet sugar cookie, you have my word that I will let her go, so long as you give me what I want."

I was afraid to ask. But he kept silent, *forcing* me to ask.

"What do you want?"

"I want Alexander. He has been playing a childish game with me for too long now, and it has become a nuisance."

"You want to exchange Alexander for Chrissy."

"Yes. But he must allow me to tie him up before I will exchange her."

"You're afraid to fight him."

He gave a soft chuckle. "No, but I confess, I'd rather save myself the trouble and have him at my mercy."

He didn't just want to kill Alexander, I realized. He wanted to torture him. "Alexander will never give himself up."

"He would to save an innocent. Didn't he give up the chance to kill me in order to save you the other night?"

I didn't answer. I heard an odd sound in the background, on Vigo's end. A faraway, tinny sort of voice, as if someone were making an announcement, followed by a ping. I strained to hear better, but Vigo spoke again.

"If he was willing to give me up to save you, my dear, I imagine he'll want to save your sister. She is a pretty enough girl, your Chrissy, though not as pretty as you. And her choice of attire is questionable."

"If you really want to have Alexander at your mercy," I offered in desperation, "you'd exchange Chrissy for me instead."

"Hmm, that's a thought. Still, it would only delay the inevitable. I am quite convinced your sister is enough. Alexander had a sister, you know. But she was small, not a full meal in and of herself. Thankfully, his parents—"

"Stop!" I shouted. I had to lean on Katie for support.

"Your nerves are as brittle as your sister's, I see. Would you be kind enough to pass the message on to Alexander for me? Either that, or give me his number so that I can call him?"

"I'll tell him. How can I call you back?" The caller ID just said PRIVATE NUMBER.

"I will call you at six o'clock tonight. If the answer is no, she'll be dead by six fifteen. Until then." He hung up.

Katie and I stared at each other.

Something clicked in my mind. That sound. I knew that sound.

"He's at the Atrium Mall," I said.

"How can you know that?"

"I heard a PA announcement. He must've gone there because his hideout is underground and wouldn't have phone reception."

"Couldn't it be any mall, or a bus or train station? Lots of places have PA systems."

"At the end of the announcements, I heard a *ping*. They do that at Waldo's when they're having a blue light special. The only Waldo's is at the Atrium Mall. I've seen the underground schematics. There are lots of tunnels under there. He must be holding her nearby. If not in the main tunnels, in one of the offshoots."

"You have to call Alexander," Katie said.

"Right." When I went to dial the phone, my hands were shaking.

There was no answer. I wasn't surprised. He must have been underground. I left a message. "Vigo called. She's alive. I'm sure he called from the Atrium Mall. I'm heading there now. We need to find Chrissy before he calls again at six o'clock."

Katie eyed me carefully. "You didn't tell him about the offer."

"I know."

"It's not your decision to make. It's his."

"If we don't find her by then, I'll tell him." I was already in motion, grabbing my knapsack. I went to the kitchen and packed a flashlight and a butcher's knife, for all the good they would do.

"You can't kill him with that," Katie pointed out.

"I know. But it's all I've got. Even if I had a stake, I'm not strong enough to drive it through his rib cage. He won't just melt away like on TV."

"*I'm* strong enough," Katie said.

I shook my head. "You're not going with me."

"You need my help and you know it, so don't waste time arguing. But I'm not going without something I can kill him with."

"We're not trying to kill him, we're just trying to locate him. Once we figure out where they are, we'll call Alexander."

"Alexander isn't answering his phone. He could be in a tunnel miles away."

"Then we'll get the police."

"The police won't know how to kill him."

"They don't have to. We just need them to distract him so that we can get Chrissy out of there."

"Fine, but I still want to bring a stake," she insisted. "We'll drop by my place on our way."

"You have a stake at your place?"

"No, but the next best thing."

$\mathcal{S}$ixteen

WE RAN TO KATIE'S PLACE, where she grabbed a hockey stick and broke it over her knee. "Here's our stake." She tucked the sharper half into my knapsack with the tip face down.

By 2:47 p.m., we were at the mall.

My phone buzzed. It was Alexander.

"Where are you?" I asked.

"I am almost at the mall." It sounded like he was running. I heard a car horn blare.

"We'll meet you in the basement in front of Michaels Crafts," I said.

Five minutes later, he joined us. He wore his long coat. He had a stake in there, I knew. Maybe several. When he shot a suspicious glance at Katie, I explained that she had been filled in — and was trustworthy. Alexander looked dubious, but nodded.

"Two days ago I followed the tunnels north," he told us. "Vigo would not be hiding there unless he moved last night, and I doubt he had the time to do so. He would take her where he had already established a hiding place. We'll go south and check the offshoots. Follow me."

He led us to a maintenance door. We blocked him from view as he jiggled a small metal gadget in the lock until it clicked open. Then we all slipped inside and down a staircase. He opened another door, and we entered the darkness of the tunnel.

It was cold. I felt the crunch of dirt underneath my feet. My eyes slowly adjusted until I saw the ground beneath me and a long, curving tunnel ahead. Every few yards there was a maintenance light attached to the wall, a beacon for city workers who came down here.

Katie and I started walking, but Alexander blocked us with his arm. "Not that way. This way." He switched on his flashlight for a second, and it revealed a cavelike passageway to our left. My throat constricted, but I didn't back away. We had to find Chrissy.

"Follow me by sound," he whispered. "Don't use your light unless I tell you."

Follow him by sound.

One step at a time.

One step after another.

After a few minutes, Alexander came to a sudden halt. Katie bumped into me, stepping on the back of my shoe. I felt her hockey stick jam against my ribs, but I didn't let myself grunt. At least I knew it was sharp.

"Look." Alexander flickered his flashlight, which allowed us to see that the tunnel branched off in several directions. We could keep going straight, or turn right or left.

"This tunnel likely goes forward a few miles," he surmised. "Passageways like this one always have a purpose. They are used by bootleggers in my world. The same was true here."

"Which way should we go?" I asked him.

"Vigo prefers left. It is in the books."

Our pace was slow, our steps careful. There was no margin for error. It would be a mistake to cough or stumble. I heard breathing: mine, Alexander's, Katie's. It felt like the walls around us were breathing, too.

The darkness got softer until it became a deep grey. I didn't know if my eyes were still adjusting or if I was imagining it, but the darkness appeared to be getting lighter. I felt Katie squeeze my arm, and I knew she was thinking the same thing.

Alexander stopped. He whispered, "I hear them."

It must have been his keen hunter's hearing, because I couldn't hear anything above the sound of my breathing.

As we continued to move forward, I began to see something take shape ahead. I could faintly make out the outline of a door with light seeping through the edges.

"Unless the door is dead-bolted, I should be able to get through," Alexander said. "I'm going to rush him. Get Chrissy out and run back this way. Don't stop for anything. Now stay close behind me. It's about fifteen steps."

Fifteen steps until we were within reach of Chrissy. My pulse pounded in my ears.

Just five more steps. Then there was a burst of sound, and the door was gone. Alexander had slammed it open. He was in the room now.

Katie and I ran in. In the corner of my vision, Alexander and Vigo were fighting. The sounds of grunting and punching filled the room. Thirty seconds. Alexander had thirty seconds.

Chrissy — where was Chrissy? All of my senses took in the room at once. Small, cluttered, dirt floor, table. I spotted her lying on the floor, face down. I ran up, turned her over. It was a corpse.

"Amyyyy!"

She was at the far end of the room, a figure struggling in the shadows. Katie got to her first. Chrissy's hands and ankles were bound with rope. Katie took the butcher's knife from my knapsack and sawed at the rope holding Chrissy's ankles. It came free. We pulled her to her feet and ran for the door.

Alexander flew in front of us, thrown by Vigo. Chrissy stumbled over him, but managed to keep going. Katie sprawled, the hockey stick skidding out of her hand. She scrambled to her feet, but Vigo grabbed her, hoisting her across his chest like a shield and dragging her back into the shadows.

"You never did play fair, Alexander," Vigo snarled. "I offered you a fair exchange and you ambushed me. Very well. It'll be this one instead of the other one."

Alexander rolled to his feet, blood streaming from a gash on his hairline. I wanted to rush over and help him, but I was frozen to the spot.

"What exchange?" Alexander spat angrily.

Vigo looked at me, cocking a brow. "Indeed? She didn't tell you that if you handed yourself over to me, we could have avoided this? Tsk, tsk, little girl. Well, it is too late now. I expect this one will do." Vigo sank his teeth into Katie's neck.

I screamed, running at them. Alexander caught my waist, yanking me back. "Don't get close to him!"

I stopped, watching Katie's face contort in agony. She didn't scream. She *couldn't* scream. I was racked with terror for my friend.

Vigo pulled back. "A love bite for now."

Alexander took a step closer to him. "I'll give myself up, Vigo. Let the girls walk out of here." He dropped his stake on the floor.

What was Alexander doing? Why didn't he just lunge at him?

But I knew why. It would take him at least a second to cross the room to Vigo and Katie. In that second, Vigo could kill her.

Vigo's eyes fixed on him. "Take off your coat. I expect you have an arsenal in there."

Without hesitation, Alexander started unbuttoning his coat.

"You always take the same *direction*, don't you, Vigo?" Alexander took off his coat and tossed it aside. You could hear solid objects hitting the ground.

"Which direction do you mean – the murderous one? What other direction should I take – diplomacy?" Vigo cackled. "Now your shoes," he commanded. "I've known you to hide weapons there, too."

Looking defeated, Alexander bent down, taking off one shoe,

then another. One sock, and then he grabbed something on the ground and threw it forward with lightning speed.

My heart stopped. The stake was going to hit Katie, not Vigo!

But at that moment she ducked to the right. It was enough. The stake caught Vigo in the forehead, causing him to howl and lose grip of her. Katie wrenched away. He lunged to grab her again, but only caught her shirt. And then she was gone, scrambling out of the door.

I was right on her heels, running through the tunnel. I shot a glance back. Alexander wasn't behind me.

I heard the sound of stumbling up ahead. "Get up, Chrissy!" Katie shouted. "Almost there!"

Then they were running again, two shadowy figures in the darkness. Katie didn't forget where the turn was, thankfully. We ran down the tunnel until we spotted the maintenance door. We piled back inside the mall, closing the door behind us.

Katie pressed her hand to her neck, blood covering her fingers. She was pale and sweating. "Where's Alexander?"

"Killing Vigo." I hoped I was right.

At the police station, I insisted on going in with Chrissy when she was being questioned. Mom was on her way, but the police weren't willing to wait for her, not when their suspect was getting away. A horde of cops was, right now, descending on the tunnels in search of Vigo. I'd given them the best directions I could.

Chrissy clung to me like a small child would to her mother. I stroked her hair and told her that she was safe now.

The room contained a large steel table and a mirror that I guessed was a one-way. There was a female and a male detective in the room with us, Moody and Hogg. Detective Moody was the one who asked the questions.

"How did he first make contact with you?" she began.

"Facebook." This wasn't news to them, since I'd shown them his profile last night.

"He added you as a friend?"

"Yes." Chrissy's voice was quiet and childlike. I hardly recognized it.

"What did he tell you about himself?"

She didn't answer. She seemed to go into a haze.

"Christina?"

"He said he was seventeen. Went to St Mark's."

"We've seen those details on his Facebook profile. Did he tell you anything that might help us figure out who he really is?"

She shook her head.

"Where did you arrange to meet him?"

"The AMC downtown. But then he said we shouldn't bother with a movie. He said. . ." She drifted off again.

"Christina, tell me what he said." The detective's voice was gentle but insistent.

"He said he knew an underground club I could get into."

"But he didn't take you to a club."

"No. There was no club."

"I know this is difficult for you, Christina, but I need you to tell me what happened in that room."

Her eyes stared. "They were alive."

"Are you referring to the bodies we found?"

"Yes. They were alive then."

"How many people were there?"

"Two. A girl and a guy."

"What happened to them?"

"He killed them."

I felt a shudder. I wasn't sure if it was Chrissy's or mine. It must have been mine, because Chrissy was eerily still.

"You saw him do this?"

"No. I was blindfolded."

"Do you know how he killed them?"

"He drank their blood. That's how vampires kill."

Chrissy didn't say a word on the cab ride home, but hung on to my mom as if her life depended on it. Officer Moody called my cell to say that Vigo's hideout had been discovered, along with the two bodies. But there was no sign of Vigo himself.

Two bodies. That meant Alexander wasn't among them, thank God. Although wounded, Vigo had somehow got away. Alexander was undoubtedly hunting him right now.

"Can I get you something to eat, honey?" Mom asked Chrissy when we got in the door.

She shook her head.

"Are you sure? You must be hungry."

Chrissy looked towards the window. "He can't come in here, can he?"

"Not unless you invite him in," I answered. "Did you ever invite him in?"

"No." She looked at Mom. "Can I sleep with you tonight?"

"Of course, honey. Let's get our PJs on." Without removing her arm from Chrissy, Mom leaned over and kissed me. "Night, Amy."

"Night."

They went into Mom's bedroom. I stood there, wondering what to do next. Chrissy was back, safe. Katie, who I'd been texting with this whole time, had been released from the hospital an hour ago. She was going to be fine.

Only Alexander was still out there.

Dizziness swept through me. I realized I hadn't slept since . . . I couldn't remember.

There was a knock at the door. A quiet knock, but it made me jump.

I looked through the peephole and breathed a sigh of relief.

I opened the door and threw my arms around Alexander. "You're OK. Did you. . . ?"

He held me close, stroking my hair. "No, I lost him. I tried to track him in the tunnels, but he'd had an escape route planned out."

I squeezed him tighter, pressing my face into his shirt. I wanted to sob. Would this ever be over?

We went to the couch and sat down.

"How is Katie?" Alexander asked, taking my hand.

"She's OK. She was taken to the hospital and got stitches. They sent her home."

"Good. What about Chrissy?"

"She's traumatized."

"Did she tell you what happened?"

"I was there when she spoke to the police. Vigo had people down there, people he'd kidnapped. He killed them."

"I'm so sorry, Amy."

He held me for a while. The reassuring beat of his heart calmed me.

I raised my head. "She'll be OK, right? I know she's in shock. But, eventually?" My biggest worry for Chrissy was that her spirit had been broken. Right now I'd even welcome some of her old feistiness.

"I am sure she will be, although she will never see the world in the same way. Eventually, though, she will put this behind her and move on."

"You didn't move on, though."

"No. I could not. But my circumstances were different than Chrissy's. It was my family that was murdered."

Maybe it was impossible to move on from that. Maybe something that traumatic *had to* define your life.

"Aunt Helen was convinced that I could put it behind me," he said. "She suggested I visualize a compartment in my mind to contain the memory, where I could seal it up for ever. The idea sounded silly to me."

"I think it makes sense. Once Vigo is dead, you can move on. You can have a fresh start."

"I am too old for a fresh start. I will soon be nineteen. That isn't young in my world."

It was true. Life expectancy in Otherworld was low — what I would consider middle-aged — a result of the many stresses of living in a society dominated by vampires. That, and the fact that their medical technology hadn't advanced since the vampires came.

"You still have time to build a good life when you get back," I said.

I meant it, but the thought of him leaving this world — my world — was impossibly painful.

Seventeen

When I emerged from my room the next morning, I couldn't believe my eyes: Dad was next to Chrissy on the couch, and she was snuggled into his side. They were watching *Two and a Half Men* reruns.

Mom was in the kitchen doing dishes. When she saw me, she wiped her hands on a dish towel and hugged me tightly, as though she hadn't seen me in months. "I need to show you something, Amy."

I followed her into her bedroom. She closed the door and put on the news. A press conference that had taken place earlier this morning was on. The police chief was taking questions.

A reporter asked, "How do you respond to people who say your department is making up this wild explanation because you can't find the killer?"

"I'd say they should take a look at the evidence," Chief Arland said. "This was the last conclusion we expected to come to, but the evidence is clear. We believe a real vampire is terrorizing our city."

The truth was out. Finally.

Without warning, photos of the victims' wounds came on the screen. I had to look away.

The press conference continued with more questions for Chief Arland. Then it was back to Roger Thompson in the newsroom with a panel of experts via satellite.

"There have been conflicting reports of what was actually found in this man's hideout," Thompson said. "Detective Gaston, what can you tell us about that?"

"Well, Roger, the police have confirmed that two bodies were found in the hideout along with several bottles of blood. Forensics is checking if that blood came from the current victims or if it was saved from previous victims."

Vigo's Facebook photograph flashed on to the screen.

"What exactly do we know about this man?" Thompson asked another guest, a retired FBI agent from Virginia.

"Very little, unfortunately. He claimed to be a seventeen-year-old student at a local high school, but that hasn't checked out. We don't know his age, where he comes from, or his real name. I'm sure investigators will be using facial detection software. Right now, they're appealing to the public to help identify him."

"You're saying that we have absolutely no leads on this guy?" Thompson asked.

"It appears that way."

Thompson then turned to a sociology professor from NYU. "Now, Professor, a lot of people are saying that this man is, in fact, a *self-created* vampire — that he's nothing supernatural. Why have vampires become such a cultural obsession, especially for young people?"

"These days the most popular teen books are vampire books, especially the Otherworld series by Elizabeth Howard," the professor replied. "The result is that many young people have immersed themselves in vampire culture. I believe it was inevitable that something like this would happen."

Vigo's Facebook photo came up again. Then the screen split in two, displaying it alongside the drawing of Vigo on the cover of *The Mists*.

"Obviously the killer is trying to emulate. . ." Thompson looked down at his notes. "Vigo, the main vampire in the books."

The professor was nodding. "Yes, Roger, the likeness is remarkable. He clearly wants to present himself as the Otherworld character."

"What has Elizabeth Howard said about all this?" Thompson asked the panellists. "When she appeared on *Evening Report* recently, she didn't seem to know what to make of it."

"No one has been able to locate her," said the detective. "It could be that she herself is in hiding."

"The irony here is that her books will sell even better with all of this publicity," Thompson said.

The panellists all agreed.

Mom turned to me. "Was it really a vampire that took Chrissy? I thought she was making it up."

"It was a vampire, Mom. And he bit Katie."

She looked like she was about to faint. I put an arm around her. "We're safe, I promise. He won't hurt us again. We have to keep it together for Chrissy." I turned off the TV. "Don't watch any more of this."

Mom and I sat in her bedroom for a little while. I could tell she had more questions, but was afraid of the answers. "I don't understand it, Amy. How did you and Katie end up being the ones to find her?"

"We thought we'd search the tunnels. We knew we were dealing with a vampire."

"How could *you* be so sure that he was really a vampire?"

I exhaled. "I've read a lot about vampires. I know they're real."

Mom didn't say anything, but she squeezed me hard. Chrissy hadn't been the only one traumatized by the kidnapping. I knew it would take time for Mom to come to terms with what had happened.

When I went back into the kitchen to get some cereal, Dad was there, fixing bacon and eggs and whistling a tune. Dad seemed to have aged since I'd seen him last, his brown hair more peppered with grey than ever. But he still wore that same after-shave, and too much of it.

"Want some, sweetie?"

I didn't know what it was — him calling me "sweetie," or him being so at ease in our kitchen — that made me angry.

"No, thanks." I poured myself cereal and milk, grabbed a spoon, and jammed it in hard enough that the milk splashed me.

"I know it's been a rough couple of days, kiddo. But I'm here for you and Chrissy. And I want you to know: everything's going to be OK."

"Really?" I snapped. "You spend one day with Chrissy, the first day in months, and suddenly everything's going to be OK? Well, sorry, Dad, but you being here doesn't make anything OK!"

I glimpsed a flicker of doubt in his eyes, like he might actually be questioning himself. Then he looked back at the sizzling bacon, turning over a strip.

"She doesn't only need you in times of crisis, Dad. She needs you when things are good. When things are normal."

"It's been a busy few months, with the move and all." His eyes were still focused on the bacon. "But I'll be seeing more of Chrissy now. More of you, too, I hope."

I so wished I could believe him. But I wasn't going to set my hopes on Dad having a turnaround. Maybe Alexander was right; it was enough for me to tell him how I felt.

And Alexander was right about something else, too. When a person knows they've hurt you, they have trouble looking you in the eye.

A short time later, I called Katie. We'd been texting on and off to update each other, but I wanted to hear her voice, to know that she was OK.

"How are you feeling?"

"I'm loving the Tylenol, Ames. Loving the Tylenol."

I was relieved that she sounded like herself. "How's your mom been dealing with all this?"

"You know my mom. She's into supernatural stuff, so it wasn't as big a stretch as you'd think. It's all over the news, anyway. Luckily they're not allowed to use our names."

"Katie, I don't know what to say. 'Thank you' could never be enough. You put your life on the line and—"

"Yeah, yeah. Don't worry about it. How's Chrissy?"

"She's still in shock. It'll take some time for everything to sink in."

"Speaking of 'sinking in,' it'll take some time on this end, too. I don't care what some of the Otherworlders say. Being bitten by a vampire is not sexy."

I had to laugh. Katie never changed. She could make a joke even in the most horrible circumstances, and I loved that about her.

"When you see Alexander, tell him I said thanks for the tip," she said.

"What tip?"

"That Vigo goes left."

I met Alexander for lunch at a greasy spoon in my neighbourhood. We ordered sodas and sandwiches and fries. After all that we'd been through in the past forty-eight hours, it felt surreal just sitting and eating.

Unfortunately, a TV sat behind the counter, its volume loud enough that we could hear the news buzzing in the background. The word "vampire" surfaced over and over. I wished I could tune it out.

Alexander ate like he hadn't seen food in a while. It gave me a chance to look at him, to remind myself for the thousandth time that he was real.

"I'd like to hunt with you tonight," I told him.

He lifted his eyes from his food. "We've already had this conversation."

"Things were different then. He hadn't kidnapped my sister then. He hadn't almost killed my friend."

His expression was flat. "So, before this, his presence irked you, but now you're angry with him?"

I bristled. Why did he refuse to understand that I no longer just wanted to help, I *needed* to? "I'm tired of standing by. I want to help you catch him."

His eyes softened. "You have already been exceedingly helpful. It's because of your astuteness that your sister was saved."

"Then you should want my help."

He cocked a brow. "And if we find him? What then?"

"I'll keep my distance and let you handle him. Or call the police."

"You are not coming with me." He turned back to his fries, obviously expecting to shut me down.

"I'll go alone, then."

"You will do no such thing. It is *my* destiny to deal with Vigo, not yours." Something flickered in his eyes. "Besides, I cannot even trust you to tell me the truth."

I stiffened. I'd been hoping this wouldn't come up.

"Of course you can trust me, Alexander." I was tempted to grab his hand across the table, but then I saw his fist curl.

"Vigo wanted to exchange Chrissy for me, and you didn't feel it necessary to tell me."

"I'd planned to tell you . . . if we didn't find Chrissy."

"You were protecting me. You didn't trust me to deal with the situation."

"But he wanted you defenceless! You wouldn't have been able to fight your way out of it. It wasn't an option."

His dark gaze narrowed. "That was my decision to make, not yours."

"You're right. I didn't trust you. I didn't trust you not to do something noble and stupid."

"Now *that*" — he raised a finger — "is exactly why I can't partner with you. Admit it, Amy. You don't have the stomach for this. You're too tenderhearted." His chuckle was hollow. "You're as bad as James."

His words cut. It was no secret that he thought James was weak. Now he thought I was, too. Weak for caring about him.

I threw some money down and walked out of the restaurant. Elizabeth Howard really didn't do Alexander Banks justice, I thought. He could be even colder than she had portrayed him.

When I glanced back over my shoulder, Alexander was staring down at the table, a grim expression on his face. He wasn't moving to come after me.

I walked home.

If Alexander thought he could stop me from trying to find Vigo, he was wrong. I didn't need him to guide me any more. I knew enough about Vigo now to be useful, whether Alexander approved or not.

He was right about one thing: I *had* been trying to protect him. And I didn't think I should have to apologize for it. That's what people do when they love someone – they protect them.

It hit me all at once: when this was over, *if* Alexander survived, he would return to his world and I'd never see him again. That would be the happy ending that would allow Book Three to be written.

But it wouldn't be a happy ending for me.

If I were Vigo, where would I go next?

That afternoon, I studied schematics of the subway tunnels. Vigo would be nowhere near where we found him yesterday, but likely still underground. By now, he'd know that his picture was all over the news, and he'd be careful to avoid being seen.

I decided to go to the police with what I knew. Since they now accepted that they had a vampire on their hands, I didn't see why we couldn't cooperate. Katie and I hadn't told them about Vigo being the vampire from the Otherworld series, and I didn't plan to tell them now. It was enough that the police believed the killer was imitating Vigo Skaar. There was no need to further complicate things by trying to explain literary physics.

When I got to the station, I asked the female officer at the front desk if I could speak to Detectives Moody and Hogg. They were the ones who'd interviewed Chrissy, and I trusted them. The officer made a phone call.

"Wait here." She gestured to a chair. "Detective Moody will be right out."

Seconds later, Moody came over, holding a cup of coffee. She was eager to see me, *too* eager, which told me that the police were desperate for leads.

We went to the same interview room we'd been in with Chrissy yesterday. Detective Hogg joined us as I was setting my notes on the table.

I showed them the schematics and gave them suggestions as to where they should look for the vampire – basically, places where young people spent time. Since he wanted to avoid being recognized, I explained, he'd likely strike near a place where he could easily slip underground without being seen, such as an unused subway entrance. They hung on my every word. Not only was I one of their only witnesses, I had helped to find the vampire's hideout and rescue my sister. I was the best resource they had.

"I'll be looking in this area." I pointed to the downtown core. "There's a popular club called Barrymore's that has a nineties night. It's one of the few crowded places on a Sunday night. If he's looking to make a scene, he might go there."

"The couple that was murdered – we think he followed them out of a downtown club," Detective Hogg confirmed.

"Do you think he *wants* to make a scene?" Moody asked.

"He certainly tried to at the teen club," Hogg pointed out. I had told them about it in my initial interview after I came in with Chrissy. But I didn't tell them that I knew the guy who had attacked the vampire.

"He likes attention," I told them. "He likes creating chaos. Because he's been able to evade capture to this point, he's gaining confidence, getting bolder. He probably doesn't believe the police are sophisticated enough to catch him – no offence."

"We'll put extra units in the downtown core," Moody said. "There's no need for you to put yourself at risk, Amy. You've been through enough. It's also possible the vampire could recognize you. That would make you a target."

I gave a nod, acknowledging that I'd heard what she said. But I was not going to make any promises to stay out of this. "You need to know that he's extremely fast and strong," I said. "Shooting him will slow him down, but it won't stop him."

"Sounds like the Terminator," Detective Hogg said uneasily.

"Yes. He's a lot stronger than the average man, but if a few of you wrestle him to the ground, you could pin him. Just watch out for his teeth."

"We're having wooden stakes made," Moody said.

"Good. A stake through the heart is the only way you'll kill him. If I were you, I wouldn't risk bringing him in to the station. If you can get him to the ground, stake him."

They didn't respond, but I could tell they were both thinking about what I'd said.

Killing suspects wasn't protocol. And it couldn't be their official plan.

But if they had the chance, they'd do it.

Alexander called me just as the last traces of sun drained from the sky. I knew he was checking up on me, so I didn't answer. I had my mission tonight, and I didn't need him to help me carry it out. It was freeing and frightening at the same time.

Around nine, I said good night to Mom and Chrissy, who were in the living room watching TV. I knew that I'd never get Mom's permission to go out in search of Vigo, so I had to do it without her knowing.

In case I decided to go into a club, I put on a lot of make-up and a black dress with spaghetti straps. I even blew my hair out to make myself look older. I figured that Vigo wouldn't go somewhere with a doorman checking ID, though. He looked young enough to get stopped. Vigo would want a low-key place he could quietly slip into.

I opened my window and climbed on to the fire escape. It was old and squeaky, but I managed to climb down without any trouble.

By the time I got off the bus downtown, my watch read 9:32. The line at Barrymore's dance hall for '90s night stretched half a block.

The night was cool, and the breeze whipped my hair in front of my face. I stood under an awning outside a deli, watching the crowd. They were well-dressed twentysomethings and obviously die-hard partiers – they had to be if they were going clubbing despite police warnings about a real vampire prowling the streets. I wasn't sure if they were brave or stupid. Either way, they seemed restless in the line, constantly looking over their shoulders.

The police hadn't instituted a curfew yet, but everyone knew it was coming if the vampire wasn't caught soon. In Otherworld, the curfew for humans was nightfall. People arranged their whole lives so that they were home by then. When medical emergencies happened in the night, most people were afraid to visit the hospital, and many died as a result.

Only a few souls in Otherworld circulated after dark. They were the rebels, the vampire stalkers . . . people like Alexander.

I saw two cop cars parked on the side of the road opposite the bar. The cops knew that Vigo could easily show up here tonight, and not just because of my advice. It was obvious that if he wanted to find a crowd, it would be here. I bet they had plainclothes officers around as well.

Since the police had this area covered, it was time to move on. I headed down Michigan Avenue. Although there were a few people walking on the other side of the street, I was still nervous.

I could feel my heartbeat getting louder as I got further away from the crowds and the police.

My hand closed around the Mace in my coat pocket. I'd bought it this afternoon because I figured it was my best defence if I encountered Vigo. It could blind him for a second or two, giving me the edge I needed to get away. I had Detectives Moody's and Hogg's numbers programmed into my cell.

Suddenly I noticed two people crossing the street towards me. A guy and a girl, deep in conversation. I froze.

The guy was blond, but he had bold, striking features, nothing like Vigo's smooth, innocent face. Broad-shouldered and tall, he had a unique style with his long coat and leather boots.

I felt a prickle of recognition.

The girl beside him had porcelain skin and a halo of blonde hair. She wore a simple brown coat tied at the waist, with a white dress extending to her knees.

Before I could process it, I found myself hurrying up to the couple.

"James? Hannah?"

Eighteen

They stopped in their tracks and stared at me.

"What did you say, girl?" she asked.

"You're James and Hannah, right?"

They looked at each other. "And who might you be?" James inquired.

"I'm Amy, a friend of Alexander's."

James's eyes went big, and then he smiled. Hannah smiled, too, but she kept her mouth closed. I saw the slight bulges of fangs beneath her cheeks.

"Good God, do you know where my cousin is?" James asked, his handsome features etched with worry.

"I have his phone number. I can call him right now."

They both looked shocked when I pulled a cell phone out of my pocket. I got Alexander's voice mail. "Hi, Alexander. Your cousin is here and he wants to talk to you. Call me back."

"Any notion of where he could be?" Hannah asked.

I looked from one to the other, knowing that I could trust them. Even more so than Alexander, *these* were the good guys of Otherworld.

"He's probably underground hunting Vigo."

"Good," Hannah said. Her statement surprised me. Hannah had a complicated relationship with her brother. The books made it clear that she still cared for him despite his incredible cruelty towards humans. They had been through a lot together since that night three hundred years ago when they had been attacked and changed into vampires.

"You found the portal," I said, stating the obvious.

"Not on purpose," Hannah told me. "We spent day after day looking for Alexander or his. . ." She didn't finish the sentence. "Then today we found ourselves in an unfamiliar Chicago."

James nodded. "We deduced that Alexander must have gone through the portal, too. We did not know until we happened upon today's newspaper that Vigo was also here."

"Alexander chased Vigo through the portal," I explained. "You're in a different dimension. It's basically how your Chicago would have been if the vampires hadn't come."

"An evolved Chicago!" James turned to Hannah. "This proves how different our world would be if there were peace between humans and vampires."

I wasn't sure if I should tell them about the Otherworld books or if it would just confuse things. Maybe grasping the dimension concept was enough for now.

"Alexander knows where the portal is," I said, "but he won't go back to your world without dealing with Vigo first."

"That's our Alex." James was the only one who called him

Alex. "From what I've read, Vigo is terrorizing this city. People here are not accustomed to vampires, are they?"

"We've never had a real vampire before. Most people don't even believe they exist."

"Which makes it a ripe hunting ground for Vigo," James said grimly. "We must find a way to send him back through the portal or, better yet, stake him." When he said the last part, he put a hand on Hannah's shoulder. She slipped a hand over his.

My cell phone vibrated in my pocket. I opened it. Before I could say anything, Alexander shouted, "Where are you?"

"Downtown, with James and Hannah."

"Do not joke with me. Tell me exactly where you are."

"Hang on."

James took the phone. "Cousin! You have no notion how worried we were about you. I am glad you are keeping well."

Alexander's response contained some choice curses. James put his hand over the receiver and looked at me. "Forgive him. He's overexcitable."

Soon after, the blue Civic pulled up to the kerb. Alexander got out and strode up to James, crossing his arms. "So, James. Are you in such dire need of adventure that you followed me here?"

Then he hugged him.

James gave a shout of laughter. "Never disappear to another dimension without telling me first."

When they let go, Hannah stepped forward. "I'm so happy that you are well, Alexander." She reached out to take his hands.

He didn't touch her. "Your brother is on a rampage."

Hurt rippled across her face, but she recovered quickly. "We know the situation. It must be stopped."

"It's good to hear you finally referring to your brother as '*it*'."

She bared her fangs and hissed. He didn't flinch.

"Stop it, both of you," James snapped. "We all have the same purpose here. We must discuss what to do."

I realized the scene in front of me was practically a mirror image of the cover of *The Mists*. I wondered if I'd ever get used to the fact that I was interacting with characters I had followed breathlessly on the page.

"Let's walk," Alexander said.

Walk we did, close enough to one another that we could have a discussion without having to speak too loud. Alexander scanned the streets. The rest of us did, too.

We passed a group of teens hanging around outside a fast food place. "I cannot believe humans behave this way." Hannah was awed. "They think nothing of being on the streets at night."

"There'd be a lot more people out if it weren't for the killings," I said.

"Fascinating. Humans have so much freedom here."

"And someone from our world comes and terrorizes them." James shook his head sadly. "It's deplorable. Hannah, you should convince your brother to return through the portal. Surely once he hears what Leander has done he'll want to return."

"What has Leander done?" Alexander demanded.

"He is claiming leadership of the coven," Hannah replied. "He has told the vampires that you killed Vigo. At first the vampires were not willing to believe it, since there was no body. But the longer Vigo is missing, the more they are inclined to believe Leander."

"Vigo will be livid," James said. "I doubt he will risk losing everything he has built for centuries to stay here."

I had no doubt that Vigo would want to stop Leander from taking his place. Leander had done the unthinkable – declared him dead, and at the hands of Alexander Banks. For that, he would pay with his life.

"There is no telling how much longer the portal will be open," Alexander said, "or how long it will remain in that location. Vigo would have to agree to go right away. And we cannot trust him to go back on his own." He looked at Hannah. "You will need to cross with him."

Hannah looked thoughtful. "The only way Vigo would agree is if I assure him that you will not be lying in wait to attack him. Can you give me that assurance, Alexander?"

"Must I?"

"Yes. Vigo knows when I lie. He always has. I need your word."

"You have it, then. You have my word."

I knew it must have been tearing Alexander up inside to give that promise, but he had to do it.

"It's not enough," James said. "Vigo will not trust Alexander to be truthful with you, Hannah."

"What do you propose, then?" she asked.

"I will cross over with you. That way Vigo can be assured that Alexander will not strike at him. Because if Alexander does, Vigo could then strike at me."

"No, James," Alexander protested. "It's out of the question. I don't want you near that *thing*."

James stood in front of his cousin. "It is the only way and you know it."

"We cannot trust him not to kill you, anyway," Alexander insisted.

"We *can* trust him," Hannah said with resolve. "I can assure you that my brother would not attack James unless provoked."

Alexander narrowed his gaze. "What are you saying, Hannah? That you have some sort of understanding with your brother? *Kill anyone you want, but stay away from darling James?*"

Hannah stiffened, but she didn't deny it.

James spun on Hannah. "What do you mean? You never told me this."

"Vigo knows that if he killed you, I would despise him for ever. You may find this hard to believe, but despite everything, he still sees me as his little sister."

James took a deep breath. "Then we have our plan. Hannah, you will tell Vigo that should Alexander attack him as we cross over – on either side of the portal – he can kill me with your permission."

"Blast it!" Alexander balled his fists. "James, you know this is madness."

James turned his cool blue gaze on Alexander. "Not unless you had planned to break your word not to strike at Vigo."

Alexander's jaw tightened. "I will not break my word. But tell Vigo that I will cross over come the dawn. And then he is fair game. Understood?"

"Understood."

I wasn't included in the conversation and didn't expect to be. Vigo was a problem from their world, to be resolved by people from their world.

I was relieved that they had a plan to get Vigo back to Otherworld. I wanted him as far away from my family and friends as possible. But my relief came with an overwhelming sadness. If Alexander returned, I would never see him again, and I would know that he was in danger. Vigo would send his entire coven after Alexander, making him as much the hunted as the hunter.

I looked up to find Alexander watching me as if he knew what I was thinking.

"Now we must find a way for me to speak with Vigo," Hannah said.

"Easier said than done," James replied. "If we don't know where he is, how can we give him the message that you want to talk to him? Shall we post signs all over the city?"

"We could," I said, finding my voice. "If we post flyers at all of the downtown subway stations, he's bound to see them."

James gave a nod. "Good, then. Let's hope that we can make the arrangement and cross over before he kills anyone else."

I told them about an all-night print shop on the U of C campus where they could have flyers made. I offered to help them put the flyers up, but Alexander flatly refused and insisted on driving me home.

In the car, I handed my cell phone to Hannah. "Keep this, it's my telephone. When Vigo sees the flyers, he can call you at this number. You might get some prank calls from people who have seen the signs, but keep answering the phone. Vigo could call anytime."

She shook the phone and held it up to her ear. "Hello?"

I took it back and opened it for her. "It opens up like this."

"Incredible. Isn't it, James?"

"I will show you how to use it," Alexander said. "It is not complicated."

Alexander parked the car in front of my building, then stepped out and looked over the area. When he was satisfied that it was safe, he opened my door and walked me inside.

"Good luck putting the flyers up," I said.

"They will be all over the city by morning."

I felt a lump in my throat. I wanted to plead with him not to go back to his world. To tell him that I needed him here with me.

He looked like he wanted to say something, too, but instead he dropped his eyes. "Good night."

"Good night." I walked towards the elevator and pressed the button.

"Amy?"

I turned around. "Yes?"

"With any luck, your world won't be troubled for much longer." And with that, he disappeared into the night.

$\mathcal{N}$ineteen

M<small>OM TOOK</small> M<small>ONDAY OFF</small> work to be with Chrissy. Although she would have let me opt out of school, I decided to go, more for a distraction than anything else. I couldn't handle spending the day with my thoughts.

On the way to school, Luisa wanted to know what had happened with Chrissy. I told her I had tracked down the Internet guy, and that Chrissy was home safe. I left out the fact that the vampire killer had been the one to take Chrissy. The news reports had not revealed Chrissy's name, thank goodness, and I still had to keep things as discreet as possible. But withholding the truth from Luisa was as painful as ever.

As if she could read my mind, Luisa brought up the vampire killer.

"Can you believe the cops are now saying it's a *real* vampire?" she said as the bus pulled up to school. "There were debates about it on every channel last night."

"It's pointless debating. If he acts like a vampire and kills like one, we have to treat it as if he's real."

"There's another press conference this morning," Luisa said, grabbing my arm as we stepped off the bus — she'd gone splat too many times. "I heard they're going to announce a curfew. How do you think that would work? What about people who work at night?"

"Depends what kind of curfew it is. Most curfews just keep people off the streets after a certain time. But if they really want to keep people safe, they should close up everywhere that's open at night except hospitals, police, and fire stations."

Her eyes widened. "You think they'll do that?"

"I *hope* they do that." As far as I was concerned, any measure that would make it more difficult for Vigo to find victims was a good thing.

When Luisa and I got to our lockers, I was so lost in thought that I didn't see them coming.

Someone shoved me, and I stumbled into my locker.

I heard laughter all around me.

"Oops, *sorry*, party crasher," Brian said, cackling. He had the rest of the jock squad with him – Reuben, Jake, and Tommy. They high-fived.

Something inside me snapped. As if my legs had a will of their own, I walked up to Brian. "Try that again, Brian."

He looked startled. "Try what?"

"The apology. Or the shove. Both were on the weak side, don't you think?"

Brian appeared dumbstruck. His eyes darted to his friends, uncertain of what to do next. Reuben nudged him, and they walked away. I heard the words "weirdo" and "crazy".

As I watched them go, satisfaction swept through me. Maybe I had an Alexander Banks side after all.

Luisa put her arm around me. "You rock, Amy. You totally shook him up."

"You think?"

"I *know*. You go, girl. And, for the record, I'm sorry I ever liked that loser Jake. That whole crowd is bad news."

As expected, the press conference that morning announced the start of the curfew. Everyone was buzzing about it. Their biggest concern was how this would affect their plans on Halloween, which was tomorrow. Most of them would now be going to house parties, and planned to sleep over.

At lunchtime, Katie and I watched a replay of the press conference on the little TV in Ms P's office. Luisa was at an emergency drama club meeting to reschedule their upcoming evening performances. I'd already brought Katie and Ms P up to speed on Hannah and James's arrival and the plan for them to escort Vigo back through the portal.

". . . and anyone on the streets after six o'clock will be fined or arrested," Police Chief Arland was saying. "Employers are required to let their employees leave early enough that they can be home by the time the curfew is in effect. All businesses must close by five. Only emergency services will remain open. We consider this curfew a temporary measure. We cannot estimate for how long it will be in place."

The newscaster then started to talk about various civil liberties groups that were protesting the curfew. There were even plans for an outdoor protest tonight at eight o'clock in front of City Hall.

"Those people should stay out of it," Ms P said, half to us, half to the TV. "The police are just trying to protect us. Why make their job more difficult?"

"The protest will draw the police away from other parts of the city, and that'll make it more dangerous for everyone else," Katie said. She was wearing a turtleneck that mostly covered up the bandage on her neck. When people asked about her injury, she told them that some hot grease had leaped out of the frying pan and burned her.

"I'm worried about all the house parties tomorrow night," I told them. "Some kid could invite Vigo in."

"Or Vigo could be calling Hannah right now and arranging to go back through the portal tonight," Katie said, ever the optimist.

Ms P put her hand on mine. "You know, Amy, Alexander is doing the right thing by going back, even if it's at great cost to himself."

She knew what going back meant for Alexander's future. We all knew.

———————

When I got home from school, Alexander called me.

"Vigo contacted Hannah a few minutes ago," he said without prelude.

I felt no relief. Instead, cold dread settled inside me. "What happened?"

"He is eager to go back to our world to confront Leander."

"Did he agree to be escorted over?"

"Yes. Tomorrow at sunset. In the meantime, he gave his word that he will not kill tonight."

"Do you believe him?"

"Yes. He needs us to find the portal, and he knows that time is of the essence — not only because Hannah informed him that the portal may close, but because Leander is trying to assume the leadership as we speak. So he must cooperate." He was silent for a few moments. "I have one more thing to ask of you, Amy."

"What is it?"

"Let me come and see you tonight."

Tears stung my eyes. He wanted to say goodbye. I didn't know if I could bear it, but I couldn't say no. I had to see him one last time.

"OK."

The knock came around eight. It didn't startle Mom or Chrissy, since I'd let them know that he would be coming over.

I checked the peephole, then opened the door. For a moment, I just stared, drinking in the sight of him. Alexander was the most beautiful guy I'd ever seen, and I knew that I would always remember him this way – standing in my doorway, his hair mussed from the wind, a warmth in his eyes that took my breath away.

"Come in."

He said hello to Mom and Chrissy. Mom smiled, Chrissy gave a shy nod. There was no anger in her eyes any more. Instead, there was something resembling wonder. She knew he'd been responsible for rescuing her.

"What's it like out there?" I asked. "Are many people breaking curfew?"

"Very few. The streets are mostly deserted."

Mom's head turned at the word "curfew". She was probably wondering why Alexander wasn't respecting it, but she didn't say anything.

"Are you hungry?" I asked. "We have chicken casserole. And lasagne from last night."

"I'm fine, thank you."

"Let's go to my room."

He followed me in and closed the door.

I sat on my bed. He stayed standing.

"You can sit if you want," I told him.

"It's all right. I'm not going to stay long. It'll just prolong. . ." He seemed to have trouble finding words. "I came to thank you. And to apologize."

"You don't need to thank me. And there's nothing to apologize for."

"But there is." He swallowed. "I know I am a difficult person at the best of times, and I've said some unkind things."

"I'm not mad any more." It was true. I was heartbroken that he was leaving, and terrified for his future. There was no room for anger.

"Even so. I should never have implied that you were weak when you have been nothing but courageous. I was furious with myself, not you. Had I not failed to kill Vigo, there would have been no cause for you to put yourself at risk."

I held out my hand. He took it and sat beside me.

"Your compassion, your kindness, these are your strengths, Amy. They allow you to face what other people would find intolerable."

"I don't think so. I think I'm just normal."

He smiled, but his eyes were full of sadness. "Then you are the most wonderful normal person I've ever met. I will never forget you."

"I'll miss you." The words didn't come close to what I wanted to say. I wanted to tell him I didn't know how I could go on if he didn't survive. I wanted to tell him I'd never love anyone like I loved him.

I grasped both of his hands, pulling them close to my heart. "You don't have to go back, Alexander. You can stay here. Start a new life. Isn't that what you want?"

"My fate is to face Vigo one way or another. One of us will die soon. I feel it."

My eyes burned with tears, and I wrenched my hands from his. "You don't get it, do you? You're wasting your life, Alexander. Your family might have died, but you didn't! There's still time for you."

He touched my cheek, catching a tear on his thumb. "Now that I know what it is to love, I won't feel my life has been wasted."

I fell into his chest and his arms encircled me. He laid his cheek against the top of my head. I wanted to stay in his arms for ever. But eventually I felt his hold loosen, and he eased away. "I must go." He rose to his feet.

So did I. "Goodbye, Alexander."

He pulled me against him and kissed me. I kissed him back with a longing that had been building inside me since I first read about him in the pages of *Otherworld*.

When we drew apart, he left the room. I heard him say goodbye to Mom and Chrissy, then close the front door.

I collapsed onto my bed, sobbing.

Alexander was gone. Gone for ever. Even though I might read about him in the pages of Book Three, I would never see him again. I would never be able to look into his eyes again, or hear his voice, or feel his kiss.

I felt like my heart had been ripped out and I had nothing left inside me. Nothing.

Mom and Chrissy came in, looking down at me with concern.

"I'm sorry, Amy," Chrissy said, and put her arms around me.

Twenty

THE NEXT MORNING when my alarm buzzed, I slapped it off. I had no desire to get out of bed, go to school, eat, or do anything else but fall back into oblivion. Alexander would be returning to his world, leaving a gaping hole in mine.

I turned on the radio and tried to focus on the news. There were no murders last night. The police announced that the curfew had been effective. I knew it wasn't because of the curfew, though. It was because Vigo had promised not to kill.

I found Chrissy in the living room, eating oatmeal in her pyjamas.

"Are you going back to school today?" I asked.

"Yeah. I mean, it's Halloween."

That made me smile. Halloween was one day of the school year Chrissy never missed. The old Chrissy might be coming back.

When I met Luisa on the bus, she was wearing an intricate gypsy costume complete with a colourful skirt and gold hoop earrings.

"I'm not going to let what's going on stop me from celebrating Halloween," she said. "Katie's dressing up, too. Why didn't you?"

"Other stuff on my mind."

"Is it about Alexander? So are you guys together or not?"

"We're not. He's leaving town."

"Sorry to hear that. Well, he didn't look *that* much like Alexander Banks, when you think of it."

I smiled, fighting down the lump in my throat.

Today at my locker I wasn't going to make the same mistake I did yesterday. As I gathered my books, I kept glancing over my shoulder. When I spotted the jock squad headed in my direction, I shut my locker and stood with my back to it. They were all dressed like vampires in long black capes with plastic fangs hanging out of their mouths.

None of them looked my way.

"Guess you scared them off yesterday," Luisa said.

I wasn't sure I'd scared them off permanently, but I was glad they didn't feel the need to harass me again.

"They're such losers," Luisa said. "I can't believe they would dress like vampires, considering what's going on. That is so tactless."

"That's the jock squad for you."

After school that day was Halloween Idol, a costume competition in the gym. I had no desire to go, but Katie and Luisa begged me. They weren't participating, but they insisted it would be fun to watch. Luisa was still in her gypsy costume, and Katie was Little Bo Peep in a pink polka-dot dress. Her blonde hair was in pigtails, and she carried a shepherd's staff. She'd covered the bandage on her neck with a polka-dot scarf.

Reluctantly, I followed my friends to the gym, where the contest had already kicked off. Everyone was crowded around the catwalk that jutted out from the stage, cheering the contestants. Music boomed from the speakers, and judges — a group of popular senior girls — held up score cards.

Luisa, Katie, and I hung near the far west wall. It was too loud to do much talking, so we just watched the show.

A girl dressed as an anime character strutted down the catwalk. Her costume was clever — a Japanese wig, a bright red minidress, and knee socks with multicoloured stripes.

My eyes took in the crowd. I noticed that a third of the people here were dressed as vampires. Reuben and his friends weren't the only tactless people at this school.

In fact, the next contestant was dressed like a vampire, too. He wore a spiked collar, face powder, and black lipstick. Katie, Luisa, and I rolled our eyes at one another.

The following guy was more original. He was dressed like a leprechaun, green outfit and hat and all. He skateboarded down the catwalk. I didn't get the connection. I guess he was a skateboarding leprechaun.

A guy dressed as an Egyptian king emerged from the crowd and walked right up to Luisa. He wore a black robe and a gorgeous black and gold mask that must have cost a fortune. I figured she knew him, because they started talking.

"Who's that?" I asked Katie.

"Don't know." She leaned over to Luisa. "Who's your friend?"

Luisa's cheeks were flushed. "He won't tell me."

Katie tapped him on the shoulder. "Nice mask."

The Egyptian king turned to Katie and lifted his mask off, revealing silver-blond hair and pale eyes. "I believe we have met before. Do you remember?"

Then he turned to me, ice blue eyes almost translucent. "Hello, Amy." Before I could respond – or scream – he caught my shoulders and shoved me into the wall so hard I thought my spine would shatter. I couldn't breathe.

Vigo's pupils dilated as he stared at me. "Your beloved Alexander will be disappointed to know that I killed you slowly. That I had plenty of time to drink of you first." He smiled, his fangs gleaming like knives. When he leaned in close, I braced for a sharp pain, but instead felt the touch of soft, cold lips on my neck. He was tasting my skin first. I struggled to get away, but he had me caged with my arms pinned to my sides. I heard Katie and Luisa screaming for help, but the crowd around us was focused on the catwalk, cheering for the latest contestant.

"What is it about you that turned Alexander into a fool?" he asked.

Just then, white-hot pain seared me. My vision blurred. I felt an excruciating pull as he drew my blood to the surface.

No!! I wanted to kick and yell and punch, but I couldn't move. Screaming, horrific screaming, filled my ears. I didn't think it was mine.

Suddenly a thump reverberated through Vigo, and then another. He jerked away from me. Katie was smashing his head with her Little Bo Peep staff. By then, the crowd noticed what was going on, and the gym was in chaos. Some people began to push and shove, frantically trying to run from the scene, while others pressed closer for a better view. Vigo turned around and snatched the staff from Katie's grip so hard she went flying.

Freed from Vigo, I tried to dive away from him, but he caught my shirt, hauling me up. I saw his head duck towards my neck—

Then a pair of hands grabbed Vigo from behind, yanking him back and slamming him to the floor.

Alexander.

Vigo kicked out with his legs, but Alexander had him flat on his back. Pinning Vigo with his body, he twisted his arms and legs in a wrestling hold. Vigo let out a howl of agony.

In a lightning-quick movement, Alexander pulled out the stake and raised it over Vigo's chest. I held my breath.

Neither of us saw them coming.

The jock squad leaped at Alexander, dragging him off Vigo and shoving him to the floor. They had obviously recognized him as the guy who'd crashed Brian's party, and saw their chance to take revenge.

Katie, Luisa, and I tried to grab hold of the guys' arms to pry them off Alexander, with no success. Alexander kicked a leg out, connecting with Jake Levine's shin. Jake cried out in pain and staggered back, and Alexander used the space to roll out from under them. He jumped to his feet.

"Where'd he go?" Alexander shouted.

Katie answered by pointing to the other end of the gym.

Alexander snatched the stake off the ground and sprinted across the gym. I ran after him. So did Katie and Luisa. And so did the jock squad.

I spotted Alexander and Vigo at the far end of the hallway. They were slamming each other into the lockers so fast that I couldn't tell who was in control of the fight. The jocks were already there, but Alexander and Vigo were thrashing too violently for them to pounce again.

I ran up, Katie and Luisa beside me. We felt helpless to do anything. Alexander's stake had fallen to the floor. *Thirty seconds. Thirty seconds before he tires and Vigo takes advantage.*

Glass smashed. The fire alarm wailed. Reuben had broken the glass and was pulling out the heavy fire extinguisher. Brian helped him.

Katie and I looked at each other. If the spray was powerful enough, it could stun both Vigo and Alexander for a few seconds. That would give Katie enough time to stake Vigo.

Reuben hefted the fire extinguisher. "Hold him still!"

I realized, with horror, that spraying them wasn't Reuben's plan at all.

We ran at him, but he'd already sprung forward. I heard a sickening thud as the fire extinguisher connected with Alexander's head. Alexander sank down against the lockers.

Vigo gave Reuben a satisfied smile. "Why, thank you." Then he sank his fangs into his neck. Reuben's eyes were wide and staring, but he didn't struggle.

Brian ran up, grabbing Vigo's robe. Tommy and Jake stood nearby, paralysed with fear. Vigo turned a furious gaze on Brian, pushing Reuben aside. In one vicious movement, he headbutted Brian, who crumpled to the floor like a rag doll.

I hadn't noticed that Alexander had got to his feet. To me, he appeared as if out of nowhere, rising behind Vigo like a cloud of darkness. Alexander lunged forward, and I heard the sickening crunch of shattered bone. I didn't even see the stake until its tip thrust out the front of Vigo's rib cage.

The vampire fell.

There was no struggle, no writhing. No spiteful last words. He died instantly.

Only then did I start to feel it – the ache in my neck, the weakness throughout my body. I pressed a hand to my neck, but the stickiness of the blood made me yank it back. Within moments Katie and Luisa were by my side, and Katie was pressing something soft, maybe her scarf, against my neck.

Alexander came up and put his arm around me. I sagged into his side. He replaced Katie's hand on my neck wound, keeping firm pressure on it as we walked in the direction of the exit.

I heard police sirens getting closer. Music still blared in the gymnasium.

But one haunting sound rose above the others.

It was the sound of Reuben sobbing.

$\mathcal{T}$wenty-one

IN THE HOSPITAL, I told Luisa everything, with Katie filling in the parts that I was too weak to explain. Luisa was stunned and furious and relieved that I was OK — leave it to Luisa to experience so many emotions all at once. She sat by my side and held my hand as I got stitches in my neck. Luckily, the hospital staff didn't pay any attention to our conversation.

Next, the police came. Alexander had disappeared after dropping me off at the hospital. Although he was the hero who had stopped the vampire killer, he couldn't tell the police who he really was. I answered a few questions, but insisted I hadn't seen who had staked Vigo.

By the time Katie, Luisa, and I left the hospital, it was dark outside. Luisa's dad picked us up. On the drive home, we saw that the streets were flooded with people celebrating. Word must have got out that the vampire who'd been terrorizing the city was dead. There was no fear any more. Everyone wanted to party. It was Halloween, after all.

I'd called Mom from the hospital and given a brief

explanation: the vampire was dead and I was fine. When I got home, she and Chrissy surrounded me with hugs.

"Are you sure he's dead?" Chrissy asked.

"Yes. I saw him staked. Alexander killed him."

"What a remarkable young man," Mom said, and Chrissy nodded in agreement.

I went to my room to change. My shirt was covered in dried blood. Instead of putting it in the laundry basket, I put it in the trash. I never wanted to see it again.

I had an overwhelming urge to shower, but I didn't want to get the stitches wet, so I used a cloth to clean myself up in the bathroom, then I put on fresh clothes. I saw the purple bruises on my arms where Vigo had held me, and I flashed back to those seconds of terror.

The door buzzer went off, followed by a knock a couple of minutes later. I knew who it would be.

When I came into the living room, Mom was hugging Alexander and thanking him profusely. I heard Chrissy say that he could stay here any time he wanted, and she would give him her room. Alexander looked embarrassed by their gratitude, and relieved to see me walk in.

"Amy. Do you feel well enough to go out for dinner?"

"Sure." It was true; now that I was home and safe, I felt almost normal again. And I was starving.

"Excellent."

When we stepped outside, the chilly air hit me. It was cold enough to see your breath, and I remembered another frosty Halloween years ago when Mom had tried to fit my costume over my winter jacket. I was glad that there would be trick-or-treating tonight.

When we got into the car, he didn't immediately turn on the ignition. "I am obliged to you."

"For what?"

"For agreeing to go on a date with me."

I smiled. Our first real date. It was about time.

First and last. My heart ached. It wasn't going to be easy to spend the next few hours with him, knowing that he would be leaving soon. But we wouldn't be parting in despair, not any more. There was hope for Alexander. Hope for all of Other world. If Vigo could be defeated, so could Leander. Good had conquered evil in my world, and it could in Alexander's as well.

"Where are we going?" I asked.

"I have somewhere in mind."

He drove past a group of teens running along the sidewalk, shouting as if their school had just won a sports championship. Their exuberance made us laugh.

"It's because of you, Alexander. You made this possible."

"Too many people have died to celebrate this as a victory. I am glad it's over."

"Me, too." It was the biggest understatement imaginable. "Where are James and Hannah?"

"Dining downtown. I thought we could join them later. They wish to make the most of their last night here."

"Did you ever tell James and Hannah about the Otherworld books?"

"Yes, and they accepted it far more readily than I did," he said wryly. "I suppose going through the portal had already thrown their sense of reality to the winds. In fact, I think they rather enjoyed the idea of being in those books. You should have seen their faces when they saw the displays at the bookshop."

"I can't blame them. I'm sure I'd get a kick out of it."

When I saw that we were heading for the river, I felt tears come to my eyes. I blinked them back, determined to enjoy every moment of this night.

The place was called Ella's. It was located on the river's edge and had twinkling lights lining the roof. I'd never been here before.

"They might have a dress code." I looked down at my jeans.

"If they don't let you in, I'll—" Then he smiled. "I won't make a scene. I'll simply drive us somewhere else."

"Let's give it a try, then."

The inside of the restaurant was country elegant with maritime fishing scenes mounted on the walls. It was darker than I was used to, mainly illuminated by candlelight. Because it was so packed with customers, we didn't get to sit by the windows, but were shown to a cosy corner table.

We ordered sodas, and the waiter came back soon after with a loaf of bread covered by a cloth. Alexander cut a few slices. "It's still hot."

I spread some butter on my slice. It tasted heavenly. "Nice place."

"You've never been here before?"

"No."

"I asked a few strangers where a nice place to take a date would be. Several said here."

I blushed. "You didn't need to go to that trouble. I'd be happy anywhere."

"I know."

I took a few more bites of bread. "I haven't been able to get it off my mind. . . You knew what Vigo planned to do, right? That's why you were at my school."

"Yes. Vigo knew how I felt about you. He's no empath, that is certain, but there was clear evidence of what was between us." His eyes glittered with warmth. "I gave up the chance to kill him to prevent you from being shot by the police. And you refused to ask me to exchange myself for Chrissy. What better way to destroy me than to kill the woman I love?"

He loved me. He *loved* me. I still couldn't believe it. It was what I'd dreamed about from the moment I'd met him in the books. But it wasn't the book character who loved me, it was Alexander himself.

His dark gaze met mine. "Vigo killed all of the people I loved as a child. And he planned to kill the woman I love now that I am a man. It would be an exquisite tragedy, and nothing would have pleased him more."

"How did you know he was going to strike at the school?"

"Once I studied the schematics of your school and the surrounding tunnels, I became convinced of it. He would have been able to go from the tunnels through the boiler room and into the basement, then take an elevator to any floor of your school. I knew he would have a costume of some kind to avoid exposure to sunlight." He sighed. "I thought I had it all figured out. What I didn't anticipate was that I would be spotted by hooligans and chased down the halls of your school. I only wish I'd got to you sooner."

"I'm just glad you were there. You said last night that you had the feeling that one of you would die soon. You were right."

"It was inevitable."

The waiter returned. I ordered haddock and chips, and Alexander ordered mahimahi. He said he'd never heard of it, but the name piqued his interest.

"How is Hannah coping with Vigo's death?" I asked.

He looked pensive. "I don't know. She didn't cry for him."

For once, he wasn't speaking about Hannah with bitterness.

"She's not evil," I said.

"No, she isn't." He wasn't admitting that he'd been wrong about her, but it was progress nonetheless. She had done her part to help him stop Vigo, after all.

"I figure you guys plan to leave as soon as possible but. . ." Even as I said the words, I knew it was a mistake, that I was only making things harder for us both. But I couldn't help myself. "Maybe you should stay a few more days so that James and Hannah can see more of the city."

I glimpsed the sadness in his eyes. My heart sank.

"According to Ms P, the portal has begun to waver. Leaving tonight is the safest option. The portal may not be there tomorrow."

"I understand," I said, feeling a wave of despair crash over me. "I'd like to be there when you go through, if that's OK with you." I knew that watching him go would tear me apart, but I had to do it.

He raised a brow. "Who said I was going through?"

My heart slammed against my rib cage. "I – I just assumed. Are you saying you're *not* going?"

He took my hand across the table. "It wasn't much of a life, Amy. You said it yourself. I will start afresh here, in this world of possibilities."

I couldn't grasp what I was hearing. I felt joy rising inside me. It was all I could do not to leap across the table into his arms. "I thought you felt you had to go back."

"Not any more. I've given it much thought. If I return and Vigo does not, it will confirm Leander's claim that I killed him.

That would enrage his coven. If neither of us returns, it will remain a mystery."

"That makes sense," I said, nodding emphatically. Alexander was *staying*. Here. I couldn't believe it.

"But that is not entirely the reason," Alexander added. His eyes met mine. "I want to be with you, Amy. I would like to do this again – this thing you call dating. If you are not opposed, of course."

"No, I'm not opposed," I said, grinning.

Hannah bounced on her toes as we waited in line, excited to go in and see what our nightlife was like. I wondered if, deep down, she grieved Vigo, or if she had grieved the brother she'd grown up with a long time ago.

When James and Hannah had said they wanted to go dancing, I'd suggested Club Teen Scene.

"Can I let two of my friends know we'll be here in case they want to come and meet you?" I asked them. "They're huge fans of yours."

They beamed, and agreed.

When we got inside the club, James and Hannah took in the place. The flashing lights and pumping dance music must have been like nothing they'd ever experienced.

"Where is the music coming from?" James asked, looking around.

"A . . . music machine," I explained. I doubted explaining a

DJ's role would help. "It's prerecorded."

"Remarkable," Hannah said. "And no one is dancing with a partner. Is it considered improper?"

I smiled. "Not at all. See that couple over there? They're dancing together."

"They're not dancing!" James exclaimed. "They're ruining themselves in front of everyone. How will they ever find marriage partners?"

I laughed. "All of that's acceptable here, believe it or not. You should try it while you have the chance. No one will know."

Hannah caught James's arm. "Why not?"

She walked James on to the dance floor and slipped her arms around his neck. Her movements were graceful, while James watched her with a shocked expression. Then James started to move, trying unsuccessfully to imitate the motions of the dancers around him.

I turned to Alexander. "I hope you can dance better than he can."

"I'm afraid that James is the dancer of the family. I do not dance."

"Not at all?"

"No. I've always thought it a frivolous activity."

"Well, I think it's fun." I grabbed his hand. "Come on. You don't have to do anything fancy."

He didn't resist when I pulled him on to the floor. I started to dance a little. Alexander just stood there, observing me and the other dancers.

I leaned close to him. "You should move a bit."

"How?"

"Just nod your head to the beat. And move your shoulders like this." I showed him.

He complied, doing exactly what I'd done.

"You're a natural!"

We hadn't been dancing long before Katie and Luisa showed up. They stood by the dance floor staring at James and Hannah. Laughing, I dragged my friends up to them.

I shouted the introductions. "James, Hannah, these are my best friends, Katie and Luisa!"

"Enchanted." James bent over their hands. Katie and Luisa were mesmerized.

Hannah gave them a closed-mouth smile and European cheek kisses. "We are learning how to dance like you people," she told them.

"You're doing great," Katie said, and Luisa gave a nod of agreement.

I glanced at Alexander and caught him looking down at me with a tender expression. I didn't know what I'd done to deserve Alexander's love, or how it was even possible that we had found each other across the dimensions. It didn't matter. All that mattered was that we were together now.

As it turned out, James was funny. I hadn't thought so from reading the books – his jokes seemed to fall flat on the page. But in person, it was a different story. It really was all about the delivery.

After we spent a few hours at the club, we went to a diner for snacks and milkshakes.

"That's it, I'm never leaving." James gulped his strawberry shake. "Is that not the best thing you've ever tasted?"

Katie and Luisa nodded. I could tell they were having the time of their lives. They hadn't said much all night, or bombarded James and Hannah with questions. They mostly just stared at them. I hoped this night would make up for me keeping secrets from my best friends.

"It's delicious," Hannah said. "To think, Alexander will be able to have them every day if he likes."

"I will not allow myself such excess" was Alexander's response. "Not after the few first weeks, anyway."

"I only wish we didn't have to leave so soon," James said. "There are many things we could learn from this world, so many experiences we could enjoy." His gaze rested on Hannah. "But we have work to do."

"Now that Vigo's gone, there's a chance for peace in your world, right?" Katie asked.

"That depends on who takes power," Alexander answered her.

"I am going to assert my claim to leadership," Hannah said. "If I am successful, we will have peace."

Hannah as leader of the vampires? It had never occurred to

me. Nor had it ever been mentioned in the books.

It would be perfect. As leader, she could broker a peace with the humans, and Otherworld Chicago would become a very different place. It was so perfect that I was afraid to hope for it.

"Will the vampires accept you?" I asked.

"Some of them consider me a traitor, and my relationship with James treason. But I am Vigo's sister, which means I have a blood claim."

"There will undoubtedly be a power struggle," James said. "It took Vigo years to take control."

"Vigo won through murder and intimidation," Hannah pointed out. "I would not take the leadership that way."

Alexander waved his hand. "Then you will have no chance. Vampires understand nothing but violence. You cannot deny that."

"We will make them see differently," James vowed.

"But your opponents will not hesitate to kill whoever gets in their way," Alexander insisted. "Hannah, you undoubtedly remember the terror sprees when Vigo came to power. And that was before Leander became a contender. You know he'll stop at nothing to take Vigo's place."

"I realize that. I will promise that anyone who is found to have killed another vampire in order to affect the election will be executed. But I will not have anyone killed for refusing to support me. Absolutely not."

James flinched. "But we said no violence at all, Hannah."

She looked at him, and I saw the love in her eyes. "Whether there is violence or not will be up to our opponents. If our supporters are attacked, we will need to offer them protection — and we cannot do that with mere words. There is violence in a vampire's blood, James. I believe that we are capable of evolution, but it will take time. It would be a mistake to forget our nature."

He touched her face. "There isn't violence in you, my love."

She pressed his hand to her cheek, and avoided his gaze. In that moment I saw that Hannah loved him desperately, but she struggled to fight her vampire instincts. She adored James for his pacifist nature, but she didn't share it.

I wasn't sorry to know this about Hannah. She would need that killer instinct if she was to survive the power struggle. The only question was whether James could still love her once her true nature emerged. Maybe she wondered the same thing.

James steered the conversation on to lighter topics, asking about all aspects of our world. Katie and Luisa answered his questions eagerly. I noticed that James had a special way with people, a way of making them feel they were important and listened to. That would help him gain allies, both human and vampire. But would those qualities help him stay alive when Hannah's bid at leadership made him a target?

Alexander had gone quiet. I couldn't imagine what he must be feeling, knowing that he would never see his cousin again. Alexander would have no family left. All he would ever know about James's fate would come in Book Three.

He wouldn't be there to protect James any more, and I knew that would be hard for him. But James had to carve out his own fate. Just as Alexander would . . . here, in my world.

It was time.

The early morning streets were virtually deserted, littered with the results of last night's partying. It was still dark out, minutes away from sunrise. Katie and Luisa had gone home when we left the diner, so it was just the four of us now.

Alexander held my hand as we walked, gripping it tighter than necessary. I wished there was something I could say to make this less difficult for him.

When we reached the base of the bridge, Alexander said, "There it is. We shouldn't get any closer." He was looking down at the sensor he'd got from Ms P. "It's moved a few inches."

"I see it." I wouldn't have spotted it if I hadn't been looking closely, but there was an area near an embankment that had a slight waviness to it, like when you looked down the street on a humid summer day.

Alexander and James stood in front of each other, a lifetime of brotherhood between them.

"Good luck, cousin," Alexander said. "I believe that you'll achieve your goal."

James hugged him. "I don't know if you mean that, Alex. But I'm glad to hear you say it." James took a step back and turned to me. "Take care of him, Amy. My cousin is more sensitive than he would have you believe."

Alexander just shook his head.

Hannah came up to me. "Thank you for helping us."

"You'll be a great leader, Hannah."

Alexander moved in front of her. "It may not make a difference now, but I apologize for how I treated you. I should have given you and James my blessing."

She smiled, and it wasn't the half smile I'd seen before but a full one, fangs and all. "It does make a difference."

There was nothing more to say. James took Hannah's arm, and they disappeared into the portal.

Alexander stood there in silence, unable to tear his eyes away from the portal.

"You'll miss him," I said, slipping an arm around his waist.

"Very much."

"I have a feeling that Elizabeth Howard's writer's block will be over soon. We'll be able to follow what's happening in James's life in Book Three."

"I suppose so. But it will not be easy to read about the scrapes my cousin will get himself into without being able to go to his assistance." He took a breath. "At any rate, I expect to hear from Elizabeth soon. She will emerge from hiding once she knows the threat has passed."

"I wonder if Elizabeth will try to keep you and Vigo as characters in Book Three, or if she'll have to leave you out. Her readers are going to be really upset if she doesn't show them what happened to you. I know I would be."

"I imagine she will have to do what other writers do. Make something up." Alexander turned and looked at me. "Or perhaps she could borrow from your fan fiction."

"I'm done with fan fiction." I only realized it as I was saying the words. "I'm ready to write something completely my own now."

"Do you have anything in mind?"

"Um, let's see. . . It could be about a girl who falls in love with a character in a book, and then finds out that he's real."

He lifted a brow. "And would there be vampires in this book, by chance?"

"No, I've had enough of vampires. Maybe I'll add zombies instead."

At that, he smiled.

We stared at the portal for a while, watching it shimmer as the last traces of night evaporated from the sky.

"We should go." I squeezed his arm.

"Yes. It's time to go."

"I never expected I would say this," Alexander said as we walked away from the portal, "but I have great hope for my world. I think its story will end well."

"What about *our* story?" I asked.

He stopped walking and turned to me. He lifted my chin, planted a soft kiss on my lips, and then smiled.

"Ours has just begun."

About the Author

Allison van Diepen is the author of *Street Pharm*, *Snitch*, *Raven* and the *Oracle Dating*. She lives with her family in Ottawa, Canada, where she also works as a high school teacher.

www.allisonvandiepen.com